# AMETHYST
*A Grandmother's Rings Romance*

Other books by Kathryn Quick:

# AMETHYST

•

## Kathryn Quick

Montlake
Romance

Text copyright ©2009 by Kathryn Quick
All rights reserved.
Printed in the United States of America.

Published by Montlake Romance
P.O. Box 400818
Las Vegas, NV 89140

ISBN-13: 9781477814109
ISBN-10: 1477814108

For Mom

Thanks to Judy, my BFF and neighbor, for proof-reading (since I am the typo queen of the universe) and for asking me constantly, "Well, what happens next?"

And to Patt, my other half, who keeps me laughing and makes writing fun.

*Chapter One*

A call to a family meeting.
Was there anything more rooted in tradition?
Anything more important?
Anything more frightening?

As Somer Archer made the right turn onto Main Street, she turned up the music on the jazz station and did everything she could to try to banish the feeling of dread from her mind. She tried not to think about why her mother had called this summit, but from experience, how could she help but wonder?

Since Somer's father died five years ago, her mom had been going through some changes. In the beginning all three siblings encouraged her to let go of the past and experience new things. After some prodding and poking, Tess Archer had finally agreed.

1

But in taking the plunge back into an active life, Tess had jumped right into the deep end of the pool.

A few months ago, at a family meeting, she announced she was flying to Iceland to soak in a glacier pool and wanted her children to know in case she drowned. Before that she was considering spending time with the Dalai Lama and wanted to know if they had any questions that needed answers. That was after she announced she had joined a speed-dating group and was seeing a man fifteen years her junior. Before that it was . . .

Well, it didn't matter. What mattered was that it had been their suggestion that turned Tess into a cougar and started this roller coaster ride. So even at the ripe old age of thirty-three, despite the feeling you get when the heroine in a horror movie is about to enter the empty house, fear, curiosity and a sense of responsibility always made Somer answer the family call.

She glanced in the rear-view mirror. "It's your fault, you know," she chided the blond-haired, blue eyed reflection. "The next time you want Mom to do something to occupy her time, suggest knitting."

A right turn later, she pulled into a ten-minute parking spot at the curb of the Hillsborough PD. The whine of the electric window going down sounded a lot like the ringing in her ears. "Get in," she said to the tall, sandy-haired officer waiting there. "You didn't change out of your uniform," she added as he adjusted the seat belt and settled in.

"I'm hoping that Mom thinks I'm on second shift and on my lunch hour. Maybe she'll let me leave early and you can deal with her latest exploit." Trenton Archer, Somer's younger brother and the middle child of three, had the same look on his face that she had.

"You're a detective, Trent. Whose uniform did you borrow this time?"

Trent adjusted his dark blue tie. "It's mine from my beat days. I keep it in my locker now for emergencies."

"Mom knows."

"I figured." He took off the tie and opened the top shirt button. "What do you think she wants this time?"

"Dunno, but how about we take the long way and let Ali get there first."

"She's going to kill you," Trent replied. "You've done that to her the last three times."

Somer shifted the car into gear and eased it into the line of traffic. "Then she should be used to it by now."

Little sister Ali's Mini-Cooper was already in the driveway when Somer pulled up. She pressed her hand to the hood as she and Trent passed it. "Cold," she said. "She must have gotten here a while ago."

Trent shrugged. "You go in first."

"Coward," Somer chided, opening the front door. "Mom, we're here," she called out just as Ali rounded the corner with a tray holding a pitcher of their mom's famous iced tea and a couple of glasses.

"You did this on purpose again," Ali said from between clenched teeth.

"Mooch, how could you say that?" Trent asked, closing the door behind him.

Ali's brown eyes shot daggers at her brother. "I will never forgive you for tagging me with that nickname." Trent laughed, but corralled his accompanying snicker when Ali shot him another glare. "It's not my fault that I was the 'lucky' one," she returned, emphasizing the word.

Somer suppressed the grin that always broke across her face when she thought of how they had all gotten their names. Their mom, a bonafide flower child from the seventies, fancied herself the zen-master of organization and planning. After marrying her high school sweetheart, when it was time to have children, Tess carefully planned each addition, celebrating the happy event by naming the child after the place they were planned. So she was Somerville, Somer for short, born in Somerville, New Jersey, when their father worked for county government. Trenton joined the family after an anti-war protest in the state's capital.

But Ali. Poor Ali. Somer choked down the laugh

that was starting in her belly. Mom and dad had accepted an invitation for an informal class reunion of friends. It was held at a campground in one of their favorite places in New Jersey's Northwest Skylands. Tess had enjoyed watching the children playing in the parks and frolicking in the lake so much that she and their father carefully planned their third child while dangling their feet from a wooden bridge in Allamuchy State Park. Hence the nicknames Ali and Mooch.

In those days, it was just like their mother to give order and logic to everything she did. But now, Tess seemed to be enjoying life on impulse probably thinking she had done enough planning for one lifetime. It could be a good thing, Somer tried to reason.

Ali slid the tray onto the table in the hallway and pointed at Somer. "You're doing it again. I swear someday I'm going to change my name."

"What and break Mom's heart?" Somer replied through a laugh that came out more like a snort.

"Break my what, dear?"

Somer turned. "Hi Ma . . ."

Suddenly struck speechless, Somer could only stare. Her mother, arms out ready to hug, looked like, well, not like her mother. Tess's multi-highlighted red hair was pulled back into a low ponytail, giving her a tiger striped look. Her usual denim capris and tank top T-shirt that allowed the dream catcher tattoo she had on her shoulder to show were replaced with a modest house dress and apron reminiscent of June Cleaver. A pair of sensible brown shoes completed the bizarre outfit. The only thing remaining of the mother Somer was used to having around were the bright blue eyes that sparkled with a touch of mischief.

Tess spun in a circle. "What do you think?"

"I think there might be a pod under your bed," Somer replied. "What's with the get-up?"

"Don't be disrespectful, dear," Tess replied. "I'm practicing."

"For Halloween?"

"No, for grandchildren."

"Grandchildren!" all three siblings said in unison.

"All of my friends are grandmothers and I'm not getting any younger."

"None of us are even in a serious relationship," Somer reminded.

Tess threw her arms around the two children closest to her. "That's why I called you all here today."

As she steered them toward the living room, Trent, held captive by his mother's embrace, cast a wary glance first at Ali who was imprisoned opposite him on Tess's right and then over his shoulder at Somer.

Somer put her hands up in a defense pose and tried to smother the look of shock she knew had to be breaking out on her face. She shook her head. Her mother was indeed planning something. This was not good.

Once everyone was seated, Tess handed Somer an iced tea. "Now, let's straighten out the details."

Somer sniffed the glass. "This isn't a Long Island Iced Tea, is it?"

"Lord, I hope so." Trent said reaching for a full glass and gulping it down. A look of disappointment crossed his face.

Somer looked at her brother and sister. They sat silent, seemingly content to let her take the lead. She sighed and complied with their unspoken pleas. "Okay Mom, what's going on?"

Tess smoothed back a curl that had escaped from the rubber band at the back of her head. "I just think it's time I had some grandchildren. That's all."

"But having grandchildren involves two people who are married, preferably in my case, married for a few years before children come along." Somer set her glass on the tray and leaned forward. "Trent hasn't even dated a woman seriously in years."

"Hey, wait!"

Somer waved off Trent's protest. "Have you actually looked at your condo? It's a man-cave, all wired with the latest electronics complete with a TV that's more like a wall, and *I* won't even go into the kitchen or the bathrooms and we're related! No wonder you haven't had a steady relationship since college. No self-respecting woman without all her shots would ever set foot in there. And Ali," she continued before Trent could try to refute her assessment, "She's been going to school for seven years and she's still not a doctor."

"I'm not trying to be a doctor. I'm working on my Bachelor's," Ali cut in.

"Precisely," Somer said. "And when you're not protesting for Greenpeace, you're sewing the wild oats that should have been harvested three years ago."

"What about you?" Ali said, indignation in her voice. "You're not exactly trolling for a husband. You're still trying to break the perfect story to win you a Pulitzer Prize and a spot on the evening news."

Tess stood. "Stop bickering, all of you. If one of you is going to give me a grandchild, you're all going to have to cooperate." She walked to a wooden box set on top of the fireplace mantel and opened the lid. "I have given this a lot of thought so don't argue with me." She reached inside, pulled out three rings and handed one to each of her children. "The rings belonged to my mother, your grandmother. Somer, you have her amethyst. Amethyst is said to promote calmness, something you need."

"Calmness? I'm normally a very calm person. It's these family meetings that get me all worked up."

Tess ignored Somer's protests and moved on. "Trent, yours is a sapphire. Sapphires promote harmony and loyalty. It will help you with consistency and reliability to the woman you ultimately choose to share your life."

Trent only sighed and put the ring in his shirt pocket.

"And Ali, you have the citrine. Your grandmother gave it to me on my twenty-first birthday and now I give it to you."

"I'm twenty-seven, Mom."

Tess put her finger under Ali's chin. "Better late than never, dear. It will help you get your heart's desire. Oh, and an extra added perk, it also is said to cool excess anger."

Ali's face clouded. "Why would you think I have excess anger?"

Tess reached out and touched Ali's cheek. "I know you aren't too happy about the name thing, dear. But I wanted to be consistent."

"Allamuchy, Mom?"

Tess gave Trent an annoyed look as he snorted trying to inhale a laugh. "It's a beautiful place, Ali," she defended. "How many people have such a heartwarming story behind their given name? It would be so boring to have named you something like Mary."

"But I'd have a lot less explaining to do."

Tess patted her daughter's cheek and motioned everyone back to the hallway. "So there you have it. Your new mission." She pulled open the front door. "Don't just stand there. My daughter- and sons-in-law aren't about to come knocking on my door. The end of the year is coming and time's a-wasting!"

The last thing Somer heard before she realized

her mother had even set a deadline was the sound of the front door closing behind her. She looked down at the purple gemstone set in gold in her hand. Though it looked harmless enough, Somer decided she wasn't going to take any chances.

Somewhere in New Jersey there had to be someone who could check it for curses. That's what Google was for.

## Chapter Two

Somer knew every inch of the inside of the Hillsborough Police Station. Trent let her inside before he got in his car and left. Her invasion of the police station was something Trent's sergeant overlooked because she got his daughter an internship at the paper she worked for. Each time was "the last time," but as long as she didn't stay too long, he looked the other way. Besides, she didn't do it very often; only when there was a story to be had and a series of home invasions and a robbery at the local Metro Bank wasn't just one story, it was two. Breaking one, or both, would help with her plans to move from journalist to correspondent.

She walked over to the far desk and poked around a few papers. Her journalistic antenna quivered when she saw a note on the calendar that the owner of the desk had a noon appointment with the mayor the next day. She pulled out her notebook and jotted down the meeting place.

She saw the file for the bank robbery in the top bin on the desk and instinctively reached for it. Before her fingers touched it, a large hand slammed down on top of the manila folder.

"Okay, babe, just what do you think you're doing?"

Somer bristled. One delicate brow arched. "Babe? Have we met?" Her sarcasm apparently went right over his head, which was difficult because he was tall. About six-three, she guessed.

"Nick Daultry," he said in a voice that seemed to wrap itself around her and make her think of Sedona, Arizona. She'd done a feature on it and spent a few weeks there doing research. She'd been moved by the grand scale of the red rock canyons and the open, desert vistas. His voice was like that; rich and deep.

"*Detective* Nick Daultry," he repeated, his sarcasm lost on her. "And I asked you a question."

Somer smiled. He didn't have to tell her that he was a detective. She could smell one a mile away. Detectives and reporters were natural enemies like a cobra and a mongoose.

"I'm Somer Archer," she replied, purposely not answering the question he asked. "Trent Archer's sister."

"That doesn't give you the right to go through my desk."

"I wasn't going through your desk. Everything was out in the open. You know, like the sight rule for police officers and search warrants."

"You don't have to quote regulations, Ms. Archer. But there is an expectation of respect for one's space here."

Properly scolded, Somer nodded. "You're right of course." She took a step closer to him. He didn't back away. "I haven't seen you around here before. Are you new?

The question seemed to make him bristle. "Hardly. Fifteen years on the job in New York City."

"Oh," she replied, dragging out the word. "Trent told me that Mike Sinclair was going to the city for a few months."

"Detective Sinclair and I exchanged places as part of HSCTI."

Somer furrowed her brows. "HSCTI?"

"The Homeland Security Cross Training Initiative."

"Oh, the cop swap. My brother told me that Hillsborough PD would be hosting someone." She looked him up and down. "Guess you're him."

Nick was about to comment when his phone rang. "I need to take this," he said. "Are we done here?"

"I'll wait," Somer replied in response. While he

handled the call, she used the interruption to check him out.

He had great eyes; a kind of bottle green that turned to sea mist when the light hit them just right. His hair, dark brown like the color of a good mink coat, needed a trim. Not too much though, she mused, because she liked the way it curled at his neck and over his ears. More rebel than regulation. His nose was straight, his mouth looked firm. That could be because she hadn't seen him smile yet. When he pressed his lips together, she thought she could see little dimples in his cheeks that would probably make a great smile.

One phone call turned into two and Nick picked up a folder from his desk. He jotted down a few notes before he tucked it under his arm and began pacing. Somer tried eavesdropping, hoping to hear what was being said, but Nick seemed to be the master of one-word answers.

On the third call he got a bit louder and Somer's spirits rose.

"That's great. Could you bring it right over?"

Possibilities ran through Somer's mind. A hit on fingerprints. A witness. Maybe even a lead on a suspect.

She inched closer to him as he hung up the phone. "Maybe we could share information," she said. "I've kept in contact with an agent from the local FBI office after the last story I wrote."

Nick's green eyes narrowed. "You're a reporter?"

"Yes."

Nick nodded as though she'd just confirmed his worst fears.

"And I was thinking," she said quickly, flashing her brightest smile. "We could compare notes on the robbery."

He gave her a slow, lazy smile confirming the dimples, and her hopes soared. "Maybe. What do you want to know?"

"I saw that you're meeting with the mayor tomorrow. Do you think he's involved?"

Nick just shrugged.

"Okay. The guy then. The one on the phone who is coming over. Can you tell me something about him?"

Nick nodded. "Don't see why not."

"Now we're getting somewhere," Somer said, grabbing her notebook and flipping it open to an empty page.

Nick sat down at this desk and slid the file folder back into the bin. "I can tell you that he's bringing something I've been waiting for since about five."

She rummaged through her purse and found a pen. "Evidence of some kind?"

"No, take out. Do you like Chinese?"

Somer tried for a measure of composure, but felt her jaw drop open. She clicked the pen closed and jammed her notebook back into her purse. "No, thank you," she said in staccato.

"Would you rather have a salad?"

*I would rather scream,* she thought. "I would rather have some information," she said in a defiant tone, which wasted on him because he was beaming at her.

"Sorry, not on the menu."

She'd had enough. "Tell you what, Daultry. I'm going to let you sit here and enjoy your Kung Pao Chicken while I go out and actually try to find out something about the break-ins or the robbery. Then when you're done eating, you can go back to playing detective."

The remark wiped the smile right off his face. "I don't play at it, Somer. I know what I'm doing at all times."

Then to prove his point, his eyes traveled over her with tantalizing slowness, not like a detective analyzing a suspect, but more like a man's blatant survey of a woman. The force of its intimacy surprised her and sent a shiver down her spine. She had to will herself not to react to it.

"I can tell a lot of things just by looking at someone," he continued. "Like now, I can tell that you want to haul off and slug me for taking up time you could have been using to conduct your own investigation. But I'd suggest that you keep your pretty little nose out of it until we can determine the scope of this crime."

Somer opened her mouth to respond when, fortunately for them both, the Chinese food arrived.

"I'll walk you out," Nick said.

"No need. I wouldn't want your gourmet dinner to get cold," Somer said. "But after work I'd suggest a few extra reps on the Ab Lounger." She gestured to the food. "Tends to hang around one's middle."

The comment was strictly for effect. From what she could tell, Nick didn't need her advice. He looked toned and fit like a pro linebacker. She gave her head a small shake when she realized she was picturing him shirtless, pouring a bottle of water on himself to cool off.

At the door to his office, she stopped, turned back and looked at him. He must have felt her staring because he looked up and winked. His casual acknowledgement of her made her heartbeat rise.

She slammed the office door behind her. Somer had the distinct feeling this wasn't going to be the last time Nick was going to push her buttons, both professionally and personally. He seemed to be that kind of man; confident to the point of almost being arrogant, fascinating to the point of distraction, and sexy as all get out.

The force of the office door being slammed shut rattled almost everything on Nick's desk. He had to move fast to stop a pencil from rolling off the desk and onto the floor.

"Who was that?" another detective who had just come in from the back asked.

"She said she was Archer's sister," Nick replied.

The detective whistled. "Somer Archer is hot."

"Hadn't noticed," Nick lied. He'd noticed all right; honey blond hair, eyes as blue as a cloudless sky and slim with a body toned like that of a runner or at least someone who worked out. He took all that in when he tried to put her in her place by giving her the old Daultry once-over. It usually made women blush, only it didn't seem to affect her at all.

It was her personality and verve not her looks that really got his interest. Confident women were a challenge, professional women more so. And he was up for a challenge.

"Tell you what, I'd like to go a few rounds with her," the detective said breaking into Nick's thoughts.

"Why don't you then?" he asked.

"Word is she's also a spitfire; hard to handle and even harder to figure out if you ever got lucky enough to get more than one date with her."

Nick glanced at the door. "You don't say."

## Chapter Three

From the way he paced the waiting area, the mayor looked edgy. This was good, Somer thought, watching him for a moment as he checked his watch and looked out the window toward the parking lot. Mayor Brown had a reputation for folding like a cheap suit when he was put in uncomfortable situations, and he sure looked mighty uncomfortable today. She would definitely work that to her advantage.

She gave the hostess a made-up name and feigned disappointment when she found out her "party" hadn't arrived before turning and pretending to just notice the mayor.

"Mayor Brown, nice to see you," she said, extending her hand to him as she approached.

The mayor stopped pacing and nodded to her.

19

"You're that reporter—Archer. Named after a season, Autumn, April, Spring—something like that."

His handshake felt weak. In this situation, she liked that. "It's Somer," she replied.

"That's right. Good to see you. Have a nice day."

"Actually, since your party isn't here either, maybe I can help pass the time while you wait." The mayor looked at the door and shrugged. "I'd like to know your take on the Metro robbery. I understand you were in the parking lot when it happened."

The mayor's face paled a little. "Didn't you get the press release issued by my office?"

"Yes, very precise, very factual. But it didn't have the personal touch. Would you care to speculate on why you think robbers hit a bank in a small community like Hillsborough? It couldn't have as much cash on hand as, say, a bank on the main drag."

"If you want speculation, go to the police. If you want facts, read the press release." The mayor glanced at his watch. "I have an appointment in a few minutes."

Somer ignored the brush off. "Actually it was devoid of an explanation of why you were making the municipal deposit that day." She thought she saw a few tiny beads of perspiration break out on his forehead. "Doesn't your clerk or a secretary usually handle that?"

"Usually, but as you said Ms. Archer, Hillsborough is a small town. Everyone pitches in. I just happened to be going that way and decided to help out. In doing so, I saved the secretary from a horrible experience at that bank."

"Any idea why that wasn't mentioned in the release?"

"I don't know. Maybe the public information office thought it would be best to leave that particular little detail out. That kind of detail can cause a pesky reporter to go poking around looking for a complicated reason for a simple act."

"I guess the lack of a reasonable explanation would also," Somer pointed out.

The mayor smiled a weary salute to being trumped. "Ah, but it was only a helpful gesture. Unlike most of my peers who do things with a flourish and would jump at the chance to get press on something like this, I prefer subtlety."

The arrival of Nick prevented Somer from exploring the angle further.

"Somer, we meet again," Nick said.

"You two know each other?" the mayor asked.

"Just met yesterday, actually," Nick replied. "I ran into her rifling through my desk at the station." He extended his hands. "And now she's here."

"What a coincidence," Somer said in her best innocent voice.

"Yes, isn't it?" Nick agreed. He walked toward the hostess. "Daultry, party of two."

"Three," Somer said quickly. "It seems my lunch

date is MIA." She flashed her sweetest smile. "You wouldn't mind, would you?"

"Why of course not," Nick replied, with a smile that left no doubt that he knew she planned the whole thing. "You're here and since you didn't eat yesterday, you must be hungry."

"With all that food I saw on your desk last night, I'm surprised you are."

Mayor Brown furrowed his brows. "Am I interrupting something?"

"*No!*" Nick and Somer said in unison.

"You both seem a little on edge."

"You know how a gnat flies around and you swat at it, but you can't quite get it and it doesn't seem to go away? It's something like that," Nick explained, gesturing for the hostess to seat them. He said nothing more as they followed her to a small side room. At the table he settled back into the chair and crossed his arms over his chest. "Well?" he said to Somer. "By all means, don't let me stop you."

Somer gave him a bewildered look as she took a menu from the server.

"Since you got here first and probably already grilled the mayor, you may as well continue."

She let out a long breath of air. "Oh, what the heck." She scowled at Nick. "I was going to ask the mayor if he noticed anything out of the ordinary when he pulled up to the bank parking lot on the day of the robbery."

"Good question. Slightly predictable, but it still needs answering," Nick said, approval in his tone.

Somer gritted her teeth, feeling her jaw muscles tighten. She glanced at the mayor who was looking back and forth between Nick and her and immediately drew in a calming breath. She gave her shoulders a slight relaxing shake and turned to him. "Did you, Mayor?" she asked, smiling as she waited for his answer to her perfectly predictable question.

"Nothing really," Mayor Brown replied, his voice hesitant. "But I don't go to that particular bank very often."

"No suspicious cars, familiar cars?"

"No."

"Anyone that seemed like they did not belong there?"

There was a long hesitation, a faint flicker of something in the mayor's eyes, then a shake of his head. "No."

"Are you sure?" Nick asked, pouncing on the hesitation like the seasoned professional he was. "For a minute I thought you were going to say something."

The mayor hesitated again. "Maybe there was one car that seemed odd," he finally admitted.

"Odd how?" Somer asked.

"It had windows that were tinted really dark. Just the back ones, though. It was a Chevy, I think. Black. Maybe a year or two old."

"I'll take it from here," Nick cut in, turning to Somer. "But thanks for helping."

"Is that a pat-on-the-head and good-bye?"

Nick grinned. "Something like that."

Mayor Brown stood. "Maybe we should continue this at a later time."

"Yes, without a reporter," Nick agreed.

Somer lifted her chin stubbornly. "I'm not going anywhere. I'd like to finish lunch."

"Detective, call my secretary and we'll set something up." The mayor looked at Somer. "I can see this isn't a good time." Nick rose from his seat. "No, stay. You and Ms. Archer finish whatever it is you started." He waved at the hostess. "Put their lunch on my tab." Then with a polite nod in Nick and Somer's direction, he was gone.

"Thanks," Nick replied, pressing his lips together in disapproval and easing back in his seat, "I got nothing out of this because of you."

"Correction, I know this guy. He doesn't handle pressure very well and because of it I found out there was a suspicious black Chevy in the parking lot the morning of the robbery."

"I guess we did," Nick acknowledged with a grudging look of admiration on his face.

"No one knew that?"

"I didn't see it in the report."

"There must be thousands of black Chevys in Somerset County alone. Doesn't exactly narrow down the list of suspects, does it?" Somer said, a touch of disappointment in her tone.

Nick smiled. "No, but it was a good try. And we did come away with a small lead. The mayor said the windows were tinted very dark. Maybe someone else noticed and issued a ticket for a black-out glass violation to the owner."

"I could live without any more pats on the head from you, Daultry."

"Be grateful that's all I'm doing," Nick said.

Somer was momentarily stunned by the deep quality that was back in Nick's voice. It was the same tone that set her blood to percolating at the station.

"Shouldn't you have told him not to leave town or something?" she pressed.

"No need. I have a feeling he'll want to stick around and see what we find out. You, on the other hand, don't have the good sense to take my advice and leave this investigation to the professionals."

"I *am* a professional," Somer emphasized.

"A law enforcement professional, Somer. My instincts tell me there's something wrong about him. He seems to be edgy. He might not want a reporter nosing around to find out why."

"Oh please, this is not an episode of 'Criminal Minds' here. I don't know any more than you do." She purposely paused before adding, "Yet."

"Somer, crime is not a game. Things go wrong even in the smallest of towns."

"I'm not treating it like a game," Somer snapped back. "I know things go wrong even with the best laid plans."

"Do you really?"

"All right, Daultry. Since you think I'm a menace to myself and your investigation, let me give you a few of my credentials and then you can give me yours. Are you familiar with the hospital mercy killings a few years back or were you too busy giving out speeding tickets to notice?"

Nick ignored the barb. "You mean the case that exposed Jack Hawkins as a self proclaimed angel of mercy?"

"That's the one."

"What about it?"

"It was my story."

"Yours?" he asked, surprised.

"Every UPI and AP picked it up."

"It was a good story, and it made national news, but he's now in prison for life. Not much chance for a revenge thing."

"Not everyone was happy with me. Some family members said now they had to cope with a more horrifying realization than they originally thought; that maybe they could have prevented the whole thing if they were just more vigilant. I got my share of nasty notes. I'm not as naïve as you think I am."

"I stand corrected, you're not naïve. But this case just doesn't feel right and I can't put my finger on why yet. Until I do, I don't like the idea of you putting your pretty little neck on the line to help me find out."

"Pretty nose, pretty neck. You're a charmer, all right."

"It was meant as a compliment. I do appreciate women."

"And while you're appreciating them, do you also push your women partners out of the way when you make an arrest?"

Nick's face clouded.

"Hit a sore spot, did I?"

"The female members of the force are trained to watch out for surprises. Besides, they have guns and know how to use them."

For once in her life she had no snappy comeback. He was right.

"Maybe I don't have a gun, but Trent does take me to the range once in a while, so I do know how to use one. Besides, I would never do anything that would put me in any kind of danger or screw up the case."

"I wish I could believe you."

Somer shrugged. "You'll have to."

"Let's get out of here," Nick said suddenly. He stood and tossed two twenties onto the table, leaned against the doorframe and waited. Hugh Jackman could not have made the stance any more masculine.

"Where are we going?" she asked, getting to her

feet and joining him at the door. He didn't immediately answer her. There was an exchange of pleasantries with the staff and then the sensation of Nick's hand on her elbow. The pressure of his fingertips definitely did not match the heat they were sending up her arm.

"It's becoming apparent to me that if I'm going to find out what happened, it's going to have to be with you," he said as they walked to the door. "There's something I want to check out at the scene of the last home invasion. You can go with me. We'll pretend you're a ride-along."

"Gee, thanks Daultry."

"Don't mention it," he said holding the door open for her. "One more thing, Nancy Drew."

"What's that?" she asked, ignoring the name calling.

"Try not to leave any fingerprints at the scene."

## Chapter Four

If there had been any doubt in her mind before, it was gone now. Nick's car proved he was from the City. The blue paint was faded and the many dents were clearly victims of the driving wars on the city streets.

"Nice ride," Somer quipped. "Get a good deal on this?"

"This is my off-duty car," Nick defended. He put the key in the ignition and turned it on. The engine sputtered and then started, winding down to a surprising purr. "I think NYC taxis use new cars as targets, and I didn't want to give them one."

He waited until she buckled her seat belt before moving and drove like he was protecting a Lamborghini Eldorado. She scowled as she watched him drive. The speedometer never got up above a legal thirty five; maybe that was because it couldn't, she decided after ten minutes.

Or maybe Nick was a cop who actually obeyed the traffic laws.

If Nick's speed, or lack thereof, wasn't irritating enough, his radio station was tuned to satellite radio and the sixties station where every song reminded her of her mother and the amethyst ring she had in her jewelry box. After a commercial-free twenty minutes, when Donovan's "Sunshine Superman" began to play, she'd had enough.

"What's with the music?" she asked looking over at Nick. "You're not old enough to be a flower child."

"At least you can understand these lyrics," he answered without taking his eyes off the road. "Plus, they never needed a rating on the label. You have something against songs you can actually sing along with?"

"No, cut my teeth on them actually. My mom and dad grew up in the sixties and embraced all that nondoctrinaire ideology that favored peace, love, and personal freedom while rebelling against the establishment."

Nick grinned. "Your mom must be upset that her son grew up to be 'the Man.'"

"We try not to talk about it much, although Trent likes to remind her by wearing his uniform to the house whenever possible." She tossed her head as a Simon and Garfunkel classic came on. " 'Scarborough Fair' used to be Mom's favorite to sing to Ali when she was rocking her to sleep."

"Sister?"

"Younger sister and the one of us most like Mom."

"Where does Trent fit in?"

"In the middle. Ali and I used to terrorize him as much as we could when we were growing up. I think that's why he joined the force. For self-defense."

"Sounds like a relatively normal family," Nick said.

Somer rolled her eyes. A mental picture of her grandmother's ring formed. "If you only knew."

"So tell me."

"It's a rather boring, short story."

"We have a couple of miles to talk," he reached over and shut of the radio. "I'll turn off the music."

"Okay," Somer conceded. "Mom and Dad were blissfully happy, and it kind of filtered down to all of us kids. Had a great life, grew up happy and there you have it."

"And you're not married because you can't find anyone to step into the nice world they created for you," he added.

She studied him quizzically. "Where did that come from?"

"From being a good cop. I pay attention." He

reached over and picked up her left hand. "No ring dents and no tan lines. You're a reporter and I hear that you spend way too much time at the station. So it's the only thing that makes sense. If you had a husband or a significant other, you'd be home with him or at least on your cell phone checking in regularly."

Somer's eyes widened and then narrowed suspiciously.

"Am I right?" he asked.

"You checked on me, didn't you?"

"I'm a good cop. I asked around."

"Why?"

Nick tossed his shoulders. "A couple of the guys at the station think you're cute." He tried to hide the smile that began to break out on his face, but couldn't. "And maybe I do, too."

Somer joined his smile. "You think I'm cute?"

"You're not bad for a country girl," he teased.

She reached up and slanted the rearview mirror so she could look into it. "No, I'm cute. Definitely cute."

Nick turned it back and adjusted the angle so he could see out the back window again. "Then you'll be real interested about what second shift said."

Somer held up her hand. "No, I don't think I would."

"But they were really complimentary." He tried to sound serious, but he chuckled.

She scowled. "Really good for the self-esteem, aren't you?"

"You don't seem to have any problem there."

"More of your sarcasm?"

"Flattery, actually. You strike me as someone who doesn't care what people say."

"And exactly what do you think people are saying?"

Nick flashed a smile that showed his dimples to perfection. "Besides the ones who think you're cute?"

Now it was Somer's turn to chuckle. "Especially not the ones who think I'm cute."

"They say that you're a good reporter. Good enough to make it in network news, yet you stay here and do what you do best."

"You are a good cop, Daultry. I thought about going elsewhere after the Hawkins story—*Washington Post, The New York Times*—and I mulled over the opportunities, but I didn't do anything about them. I like it here." She looked at him. "Does that make any sense to you? Because sometimes I think I'm crazy for trying to make the system come to me instead of the other way around."

His steady gaze left the road and met hers. For a second she thought she saw something more than understanding there.

"I think it does," he said, in a tone that surprised her. He gave her a sudden, tender grin before turning back to the road.

"What about you?" she asked him. "Why did you volunteer for the cop swap? After the excitement of New York, it can't be very stimulating for you here."

"The HSCTI?" he corrected.

Somer smiled. "Hung up on formalities, are you? We're a bit more casual here."

Nick turned on the left blinker and made the turn. "I guess I was just ready for a change."

"But not a permanent one," Somer probed.

"Maybe, maybe not. But I wanted to see what it's like to see the sun set over fields instead of bricks and concrete and not have to wonder how many hours until the first mugging or liquor store holdup. Even big city cops get tired after a while."

"Tired? I don't buy that. I saw the way you jumped on the mayor's hesitation at the restaurant. You're a natural. Just like me. And, honestly, I don't think you'll be content in a small town like Hillsborough. You'll go crazy when weeks go by with nothing more than kids tipping cows. There's a deeper reason you're here."

He didn't deny it, but was quick to change the subject. "How did we get talking about me anyway?"

"Because I'm as good a reporter as you are a cop."

"Then let's make a pact."

She eyed him suspiciously. "What kind of pact?"

"You let me do the police work and I'll keep you

informed of everything so you can have the exclusive."

"What's the catch?"

"You stay out of my way so I don't have to worry about you. My city radar tells me something isn't right about this case, and I don't want you to get hurt."

She snickered. "Nice try, Daultry, but I'm not a small town flower who's going to wilt when you turn on the cop charm. You're afraid I'm going to break this case before you do."

"Oh for crying out loud . . ."

Somer did not wait for the rest. "That's it, isn't it? You city boys don't like being told that we can solve crimes here in the sticks, do you?"

"No." His reply was quick.

Somer glared at him. "What is it then?"

"I've been trained for this. The Academy, marksmanship, martial arts."

"And that's why you never got yourself shot or knifed in the city, I suppose," Somer shot back.

Nick's hands tightened on the steering wheel and she felt an instant pang of regret for the comment. The car spun around the next corner on two wheels and screeched to a halt in front of a large two story brick house with a perfectly landscaped front yard edged by a hitching post fence. Nick turned the car off with painful slowness and then angled himself in the seat to face her. Tiny lines at the corner of his mouth emphasized the tension on his face and anger and pain turned his eyes a dark green. As Somer looked into them, she could feel his hurt.

"As a matter of fact, I did get knifed the city."

Somer bit down on her lip. "I'm sorry. I didn't know."

"In a street fight trying to pull some strung out punk off my partner—my female partner and one of the best cops I've ever worked with." He opened two shirt buttons and pulled the collar down so she could see a two-inch keloid scar slash across his upper chest near his collarbone. He looked down at it.

"Ugliest thing I've ever seen and I won't have it fixed because I want to remember why I got it and what I did wrong."

"What makes you think you did something wrong?" Somer asked in a voice barely above a whisper.

"Because the perp jumped us. That shouldn't have happened."

Somer swallowed hard, and bit down on her bottom lip to prevent her from saying something else stupid.

"As for the bullet, I took it in the side my first week back on duty. Someone wasn't happy about one of his g's doing five to ten for assaulting a police officer and pulled a gun on me on my way to Starbucks when I stopped to get a coffee before work."

Somer could not think of one intelligent thing to say.

"That's two incidents out of thousands of calls I made during fifteen years on duty," he continued, "and although I know I'm a good cop, I felt that sometimes I get distracted. That's why I volunteered for the cross-training; to recharge and reprogram and then go back." He turned back and faced the windshield. "It may be selfish, but it's all I got."

"I'm sorry," Somer said again when her dry throat allowed words to form. "I really am. I'm sorry it happened to you and I'm sorry for being such an insensitive jerk." She fought the urge to cry. "It's just that this story is important to me too. Maybe it's because my own self-esteem is a little battered from waiting so long for the perfect story so I can get the perfect job. Maybe I'm just afraid it might never happen."

He turned back to her. "Look, I know how you feel, I really do, but something is not right here. I can feel it. No story is worth putting yourself at risk." His shoulders finally relaxed. "Let me do my job."

Somer reached out and touched his arm. She could feel the taut muscle quiver. "And you let me do mine."

Their gazes clashed and then held. Finally he sighed. "Do I have a choice?"

"Not really."

She saw resignation replace the pain in his eyes. "Then let's go inside and see what we can find." He gestured to the house. "The third break-in happened here."

*Chapter Five*

Somer and Nick walked up a winding paved pathway to what realtors in the area called a McMansion. It was one of twenty or so similar homes valued at around three quarters of a million dollars and clustered on lots less than an acre in a development-like setting. Houses like these were popular with the average upwardly mobile forty-somethings with two-point-five children and a dog and the fifty-somethings who had just made partner.

"Where are the owners?" Somer asked as Nick swiped the crime scene tape away and put a key into the lock.

"Away until we get whoever broke in. The wife gets a little freaked out when she thinks about a stranger in her house," he said, sweeping open the door and letting Somer go in first. "As soon as the scene is cleared some cleaning company is coming in and working its magic." He pushed the door closed. "Just don't mess with anything."

Somer shoved her hands into the back pockets of her jeans. "What are we looking for?"

"I'm not sure, but something's not right about these B and Es."

"What do you mean?"

"They're sloppy, like someone tried it out to see what would happen. Plus not much was taken. Only small stuff. The big ticket High-def TV's, jewelry, some valuable art objects weren't even touched."

"That is strange," Somer agreed.

"If I had to guess, I think it's kids doing this."

"Kids around here don't do stuff like this."

Nick shook his head. "There are kids everywhere that do stuff like this, Somer."

Somer just shrugged and followed Nick around the house. It was neat and tidy, except for the recent dusting for fingerprints. Nothing seemed out of place. Even the magazines were precisely arranged on the glass coffee table in the living room. Every room appeared perfect, including the family room with the custom French doors that gave the intruders entry.

"I think it would creep me out, too, if someone broke into my house," she said looking more closely at the doors. "Every time that poor woman comes in here, she'll have the mental image of someone going through her things."

Nick came up next to her. "This is just how we found it. What do you see?"

Somer bit down on her lip and considered his question. "Nothing really. A jimmied lock." She stepped closer to one of the door. "Some footprints outside."

"Look around. What else?"

She turned in a small circle, careful not to con-taminate the area. "Nothing."

"Don't you think it's a bit odd that nothing is disturbed in this room?" He walked to the lock and pointed, being careful not to touch it. "If I had to guess, I'd say this lock was tampered with from the inside."

Somer furrowed her brows. "Don't you think the investigative officers would have noticed that?"

"Maybe, maybe not. The intruder was careful to do the same to the outside lock. The detective on scene could have thought the door somehow got jammed before the intruders could leave, making it necessary to break out, too."

"That's a bit out in left field," Somer said.

"Not as much as you think. It happens in the city often enough."

"But that would mean someone living here let the intruders inside."

"Either that or gave them a key and this was set up to look like a break-in."

Somer waved his theory aside. "Oh come on now. You don't believe someone in a house like this would need someone to break in and take things for the insurance money."

"No, I don't, and that's what bothers me."

"So what do we do?"

"We keep on looking for answers."

Since the house was perfect, Somer thought there was no sense in hanging around inside. "I'm going to take a look around outside," she said, heading for the front door.

"Okay, but don't . . ."

"I know, I know, don't touch anything. I know police procedure, Daultry."

"Did I say you didn't?" Nick asked.

Somer tossed her shoulders. "You didn't have to. It's written all over your face."

Nick checked the expression on his reflection in one of the windows. "Looks the same to me."

"That's why I recognize the look," Somer said, carefully retracing her steps out of the room.

The McMansion's back lawn rolled in two gentle furrows toward a small creek and a hedgerow that separated the development from a small preserved farm. Somer guessed the farm owner sold the farmstead as civilization from other developments closed in on him. Now what remained of the farm was completely surrounded by huge homes and seemed out of place.

Like Nick, Somer thought; a big city cop in a town that could probably fit inside the Bronx. She turned back toward the house and could see him through the sliding glass doors. She walked closer to the window, careful to stay in the shadow of one of the large oak trees that had been saved during the building process.

Inside the house Nick stood with feet widespread, firmly planted, both his hands slipped into the rear pockets of his jeans. The stance pulled his shirt open a bit, revealing a little of what Somer suspected was a well built chest. When Nick turned his head to study something across the room, Somer found his profile striking.

Maybe it was his stance that caused her to sweep his length from head to toe as he stood framed by one of the doors, but it was feminine interest that caused her to linger longer than she should. Shoulders back, chest out, athletic looking and self-assured, Nick looked like the perfect big city police officer; good-looking, powerfully built, the kind portrayed in movies or on television as the hero. Although the Hillsborough police force had some mighty good-looking officers, none of them made her look twice. But Nick had, and that surprised her. Heck, if she had been counting, the number of times she purposely looked at him would probably have been in the double digits by now.

He caught her staring at him and flashed her a smile. He did it so effortlessly that she wondered how many New York hearts he'd broken without even realizing it. The smile was crooked, more on the right than on the left side of his mouth, but it made his eyes sparkle. When he smiled, his dimples deepened, changing his face from the look of a rock-hard professional cop to the softness of a man who could send her pulse racing. Those dimples were fast becoming devastating to her persona, but somehow she didn't care one bit.

As he walked toward the door to open it, her gaze lifted to his eyes. Bedroom eyes, the women's magazines would call them, with their dark spiky lashes and that glinting flicker of self-assurance that she suspected would be there even if he were meeting the President himself.

That maddening confidence spangled out from half-closed lids as he opened the sliding glass door and asked, "Find anything, ace?"

Somer jerked herself from her musings. "Not really." She looked down at the ground so he would not see her blush when she realized that what she *had* found was something a lot more interesting to her; Nick was someone she'd like to investigate more romantically.

She folded her arms across her chest and swung her head up to look out toward the street. "I thought . . ." She stopped suddenly and took off running. "Get in the car," she shouted over her shoulder. "*Now!*"

Nick barely had time to think before his instincts kicked in and he was running after her. As he rounded the last tree in the yard, he saw that Somer had gotten into the driver's seat of his car. There was only one other place for him to go.

His feet were barely inside the car when Somer gunned the engine and took off. He pulled the passenger door shut and struggled to fasten the seat belt.

"What happened?" he asked, bracing an arm on the dashboard as he settled himself on the seat.

"Remember what the mayor said about a car with dark tinted windows? A Chevy? About two years old?"

"Yes," Nick replied as his body slid against the door when Somer jerked the car around the next corner.

"Well, a black Camaro with blacker windows was parked right behind you until I looked over at it. The driver must have seen me about the same time I saw him because he took off in this direction."

Nick tried to straighten out in the seat, but Somer jerked the car around the next corner and sent him deeper into the upholstery. "We're not going to find him if we're wrapped around a tree, Somer."

"Can't this car go any faster?" Somer asked. "Why don't you have something with more horsepower?" Somer asked as she pushed on the brake to slow down at the next corner and then stomped on the gas when she saw the intersection was clear.

"If you don't stop that, the rear axle is going to fall off."

"Stop whining and help me look. We have to find that car."

Nick began to say something, but Somer simply pointed out the window. He mumbled what he thought he remembered from his days at St. Joseph's Elementary School was a prayer to St. Jude of the Hopeless Causes and then settled back in the seat for the rest of the ride.

It was nearly midnight when Somer finally conceded that she'd dragged them out on a wild goose chase. They'd taken two quick breaks for snacks and the bathroom while they combed every street in the township for the black car. Now she and Nick were way out on the edge of town on a back road that cut through cornfields.

"No lack of farmland here," Nick said, looking at the six foot high corn stalks that lined both sides of the road.

"I think we wandered into the next county," Somer said. "I thought I saw the car come this way, I really did."

"I know, I know," Nick said, opening the car door and getting out. "If you did, it's gone now and I have an early meeting tomorrow morning that I'd like to make it to in one piece. I'm driving back."

Reluctantly Somer got out. She slammed the car door and leaned her backside against it. She folded her arms across her chest. "I was so sure we were going to turn up something at the house." She looked down at the ground and dug the toe of her shoe into the rich farm soil.

"Maybe we did."

She snapped her head up. "Do you think that maybe the bank robbery and the home invasions are connected?"

"Never rule out anything until you check out all the leads."

Spirits buoyed, Somer smiled.

Nick's eyes assessed her. "What would you have done if you caught up with him?" he asked.

Somer looked into his direct gaze. *Lordy, he has devastating eyes,* she thought. *A woman could get lost in them and forget to speak.*

"Somer?"

She gave her head a little shake. "I don't know what I'd have done. That's why I brought you along."

"Brought me along? It's my car and I think originally, I asked you to come with me." It was about then he noticed the teasing glint in Somer's eyes. "*Touché*," he said, acknowledging the tease.

Somer chuckled. "Well what would a big city

New York cop do if he caught up with a suspect and wanted to watch him for a while?"

Nick leaned next to her on the car. "First I'd make sure that I didn't look suspicious or out of place."

"And how would you do that?"

"Depends on where the surveillance was." He looked around the area and the idea just hit him. He'd give Somer a taste of her own medicine. "A place like this is probably where people go to be alone." He slid closer to her. "So my partner and I would have to pretend we were a couple."

Somer's eyes widened as she felt the heat of his nearness. "A couple? Like dating?"

"Yes. Why else would two people come out all this way except to be alone?"

Somer's heartbeat rose and she inhaled deeply to try to slow it. "Okay, so we pretend to be a couple to watch the perp."

"But we have to be convincing, or he might get suspicious." He straightened and stood facing her. Reaching out, his hand closed gently on the back of her neck.

At his touch Somer held her breath. She shrugged her shoulders, hoping to free herself from the amazing sweetness of his touch, but he began moving his fingers softly on her skin.

"Nick, don't do that," she whispered, praying to the god of corn to make him ignore her demand.

"We have to be convincing, remember?"

She dropped her head backward hoping he'd move his hand away but instead the back of her head touched his knuckles in a caress. His fingers stroked her hairline sending a shaft of liquid fire to the pit of her stomach.

"Maybe we shouldn't have come out this far," he said.

"I know," Somer agreed. "But the suspect is right over there and you said that we have to be convincing." *Did I just say that?* she thought.

Nick's gaze swept her face before settling on her lips. "Are you sure?"

"Uh-huh."

His fingers tangled in her hair so slowly that it created an ache of anticipation. Just as slowly he drew her head toward him. She reached up intending to just rest her hand on his arm but in the middle of the motion changed her mind and looped her hands around his neck. She lifted her chin, closed her eyes and waited, lips parted, heart pounding, for the anticipated touch of his lips.

But nothing happened.

She could smell Nick's cinnamon-scented breath warm on her face, feel his fingertips on her neck, but all she could feel on her lips was the cool air of the evening.

"I think our suspect would be thoroughly convinced," he whispered to her.

Somer snapped her eyes open. Nick's smile said

it all. The remedial glint in his eyes sent common sense rushing in where once only a vortex of emotions played.

"The perp is probably gone by now," she said.

"I know."

She tried to pull free, but he didn't let her. His palms slid down the angles of her neck, across her shoulders and down to her waist, where he held her fast.

In response goose bumps ran up her arms. What was wrong with her anyway? A man had never affected her this strongly or this suddenly before. Could it be the thrill of the car ride? The prospect of finding a suspect? Or, dare she think it, genuine attraction?

"We should go too," she said.

"I suppose we should."

"Then how about letting me go," she suggested.

"Oh. Right." Nick drew in a deep breath and jammed his hands into the side pockets of his jeans and stepped back. For a long moment, silence hung in the air between them. "Do you want some coffee before I take you home?"

"No," Somer replied, feeling like someone had taken all the air from her lungs. "I have an early editorial meeting." She walked to the passenger side of the car. "And you have that meeting." She pulled open the door and got in.

Nick looked disappointed when he agreed. "That's

right." He slid into the driver's seat. "You'll have to give me directions back." He smiled slightly, his dimples barely showing. "Or I can try to find my own way back and risk getting us lost for a few hours."

Somer looked at him across the center column. It was an opening she couldn't take right now. "Not a chance. For starter's turn around."

Nick's shoulders seem to drop as he nodded and did a quick U-turn.

The only words exchanged between them on the way back to the restaurant to drop Somer at her car were those having to do with directions. Then Nick followed her home and waited until she was safely inside her townhouse before driving away.

She watched the red taillights of his car disappear through the front window curtains before pouring herself a glass of mineral water and settling into her favorite chair in the living room. As she sipped her drink, she tried to think of reasons why the black Camaro would have been at the crime scene, but it was Nick's face and the almost kiss that kept coming into her thoughts.

She closed her eyes and sighed. "Go away, Daultry," she mumbled. But as she suspected, he paid no attention to her, plaguing her thoughts with the way he felt when she threw her arms around his neck and the way she was fast becoming intrigued with him.

She set down the glass and pressed the heels of

her palms against her eyes. "No, no, no. This is just another part of Mom's plan."

She nearly ran to her bedroom and ripped her grandmother's amethyst ring from the jewelry box. It looked innocent enough, but she knew better. Her mother had placed some sort of voodoo, hippie love chant on it, and somehow she had to break the spell. Warmth was offset by cold, she suddenly thought.

Racing to the kitchen, she ripped open the freezer and jammed the ring in the tray with the ice cubes. A few hours in the deep freeze should break the love hex.

She closed the freezer door and dusted off her hands in satisfaction. She was not going to fall prey to her mother's matchmaking without a fight.

## Chapter Six

A hand reached around from behind Trent and slammed his locker door shut.

"So, Somer is your sister."

Trent turned and found himself face to face with Nick. "I didn't know you'd met her." He straddled the bench set between the rows of lockers in the staff room at the station, sat down and unlaced his sneakers.

Nick peeled off his shirt and replaced it with a softball uniform top. "We met a few days ago." He threw his shoes in his locker and sat next to Trent. "Seems nice enough."

Trent swung his leg over the bench and put on his shoes. "She's my sister. What do I know about nice?" The look on Nick's face surprised him. "It was a joke, man. Brother-sister rivalry and all that."

53

Nick cleared his throat in a nervous reaction. "Oh, yeah. I know that." He rose, got his glove from the locker and slung a small hand towel over his shoulder. "She seems interesting, being a newspaper reporter and all." He put his glove on the bench and set his foot next to it to retie his right sneaker.

"I suppose."

"She must meet a lot of people."

"I guess."

"And I suppose she's really busy."

Trent stood and grabbed his glove from the bottom of his locker. "What's with all the interest in my sister?"

"Nothing. Just curious."

Trent grabbed Nick's glove and tossed it to him. "Then ask her yourself. She's catching for the opposing team."

Nick caught up to him at the door. "What?"

"Somer plays for Bridgewater PD. Usually she's the second baseman, but the regular catcher is on vacation, so she's filling in."

"Is she any good?" Nick asked, for lack of something else to say as they walked toward the ball field in the park next to the station.

"Good enough, and I'm warning you now, don't try to score unless you think you can make it."

Nick held up his hands in a defensive posture. "I wouldn't do that. I don't know her that well."

Trent looked puzzled. "I meant if you try to slide

into home plate, she doesn't give an inch. It's like running into a brick wall." His brows furrowed in response to the dazed look on Nick's face. "What did you think I meant?"

"Nothing," Nick quickly replied. "When the guys on second shift said stuff about her, I assure you that it was all complimentary."

Trent stopped dead in his tracks. "What guys on second shift?"

It was about then that Nick decided it would be a good time to join his teammates and began a fevered jog toward the baseball diamond. Trent took off running after him and caught up just as Nick got to the infield. But Nick couldn't go anywhere. Bridgewater PD was warming up.

"What guys on second shift?" Trent asked again as Somer noticed him and waved from her spot behind home plate.

"I'm not ratting on anyone," Nick said tossing his towel into the dugout. "But it wasn't said with any kind of innuendo and was meant as a compliment."

Trent adjusted his ball cap and tucked his glove under his arm. He looked at his sister. Her cap was on backward and her face was obscured by the catcher's mask. She was squatting behind home plate, most of her covered with protective gear.

He turned to Nick. "So the guys on second shift think Somer is cute or something?"

"Something like that," Nick assured.

Trent shook his head as Somer threw the ball from home to second. "Sorry, just don't see it."

It was Hillsborough PD's turn to warm up and the teams exchanged places on the field. As Nick walked to the plate to get in some batting practice, Somer slid the catcher's mask up onto the top of her head.

"Fancy meeting you here," she said tossing the ball to Hillsborough's catcher and stepping away from the plate. "I didn't know you played."

"We do have ball fields in the city," Nick replied, checking his grip on the bat he had picked up in the dugout.

"That's not what I meant. I thought you'd be staking out one of the crime scenes."

Nick winked. "Not without my partner."

Somer felt a blush creep up from her chest. "About that."

"What about that?" Nick asked, stepping back and taking a few practice swings more to get his mind off Somer than to loosen up his shoulder muscles.

Annoyed by Nick's nonchalance, the blush never reached Somer's cheeks. "I must have looked pretty silly. Eyes closed, probably a goofy look on my face."

Nick felt a blush of his own creep across his face as he remembered how soft and inviting she looked in the moonlight. Another time, another place and maybe he would have accepted the unspoken invitation to kiss her.

"I should apologize," Somer continued, "I think I got caught up in the thrill of the chase."

Jarred at the nonchalance of her statement, Nick stopped swinging the bat. "That's all?"

"What else could it have been? I mean, the adrenaline was flowing, we were just at a crime scene." *The moon was full and you looked great in its light,* she silently added. She threw up her hands. "You know what they say. *Carpe diem.*" Then without waiting for a reply, she turned and walked quickly toward her teammates.

"*Carpe diem,*" she muttered on the way to the dugout, "why in the world did I say that?"

Nick stepped into the batter's box and took his stance. "*Carpe diem,*" he said, straightening as the first practice ball flew past him like he didn't even realize it had been thrown. He turned at looked at Somer's back as she stepped into the dugout. "What did she mean by that?"

It was the bottom of the ninth and Somer had just been walked. That wouldn't have been so bad, but Nick was the first baseman. With Bridgewater ahead by one run and only one out, he would have to try to make sure she didn't get a big lead and score. That meant he'd be playing at least part of the inning right next to her trying to keep her close to first base.

As she trotted toward him, she tossed the batting helmet she had been wearing to the batboy and wondered what was going to happen once she got there. But Nick didn't say anything as she touched the base. He just smiled at her.

A few pitches later, she couldn't stand the silence any longer. "It wasn't half bad, you know," she said taking a two-step lead off first. "Spending time with you trying to find a lead in the case."

Nick tapped his glove and held it out toward the pitcher, ready in case there was a pick off attempt. "No, it wasn't," he agreed.

The next pitch was a strike so Somer had to return to first base before taking another lead. "It was actually kind of nice," she said. Nick was about a foot away from her. That's how the kissing almost started in the cornfield, she remembered. He was about the same distance away from her then. She looked at his lips and smiled. "It could have been very nice."

"Time," Nick called out, raising his hand toward the umpire behind the plate. When the umpire nodded and lifted off his mask, Nick tucked his glove under his arm and turned his back to the dugout his teammates were using so only Somer could hear him. "Can we talk about this later?" he asked.

Somer's lips twitched with the need to grin but she controlled it somehow. "Why?"

"Because all this talk about last night is getting a little distracting."

She let the smile break loose. "Really?"

"Play ball!" the umpire called out before Nick had a chance to reply.

In compliance Nick returned to his position at first, one foot touching the base, the other ready to pivot. Somer tagged up again and took a bigger lead this time.

"Did you really mean it?" she asked, inching away a little more.

"Mean what?" Nick asked, trying very hard to keep his head in the game.

Somer straightened and gave him a cocked hip pose. "That I'm distracting you?"

"You're starting to." He relaxed a little and glanced over as he spoke.

Big mistake. A few tendrils had escaped from her ponytail and now moved around her face in the soft breeze. The oversized uniform T-shirt she wore only emphasized the fact that the uniform pants hugged her curves in all the right places. She had a brown spot on her cheek from balls hitting the dirt when she was catching and it made him want to reach out and brush it from her skin. Now instead of the game, all he concentrated on was the way the sun seemed to light her eyes.

Somer saw the interest in his eyes build. "Good for me, bad for you, because I've really got to go," she said as she suddenly turned and took off running.

"Oh geeze," Nick said, as the pitcher whirled around and threw the ball toward him. Nick's reflexes seemed out of whack because he didn't recover in time and the ball sailed harmlessly right by him into right field. As the right fielder ran to retrieve it, Somer rounded second and headed to third. By the time Nick relayed the ball to the third baseman, Somer was standing on the bag, now the potential insurance run in the game. She waved to him as her teammates cheered.

"My fault, my fault," Nick said, acknowledging the taunts of his teammates from the dugout behind him. *Get your head back in the game, Daultry,* he chided himself as he walked to the infield grass. He kicked the dirt on the infield rim and set his position, more determined than ever to cut a run from scoring, no matter how pleasant the runner may be.

But as he looked over at Somer, he found it hard to focus on anything but her. She had done something no other woman had ever done. Somehow, she had gotten under his skin. She was now an itch that he desperately needed to scratch.

He spent the rest of the inning watching her across the baseball diamond, half wishing she'd score and half enjoying watching her prowl the third baseline. With foul balls and time outs, the Hillsborough PD's pitcher managed to run a full count on the next two batters from Bridgewater before finally striking them out and ending Nick's pleasant torment.

Nick jogged to the dugout and descended the two steps to the benches. "Only half an inning left."

Trent had just taken a bat from the rack. "What did you say?"

Nick's head snapped up. He hadn't realized he'd spoken out loud. "Last chance to catch up," he replied, stashing his glove on the shelf behind the benches and grabbing a bat. If all went well, he'd bat after Trent.

"All we have to do is score two to beat them," Trent agreed. "Let's hope that Ted and Mitch get on."

But that was not to be. Ted and Mitch never made it to first base, leaving just one more out between tying the game with a chance to win in extra innings or losing it.

Trent swaggered up the dugout steps. "Gentlemen, watch and learn," he said.

"Think you're going to tie the game single-handedly?" Nick asked.

"No, I know I am," Trent replied, walking to the batter's box.

Somer watched her brother approach. He partially blocked her view of Nick, so she stepped back. While on third base last inning, she watched Nick across the baseball diamond. He had moved with the agility of a seasoned athlete; skilled, fluid, instinctive. She enjoyed the view to the point of her own distraction, having barely beaten a throw from the pitcher to the third baseman intended to keep her close to the bag.

She slid her catcher's mask on top of her head when her brother got to the plate. "Nick's pretty good, huh?" she asked, watching Trent take a few warm up swings. She saw him furrow his brows in response. "As a first baseman. He's pretty good," she explained.

Trent tapped his bat on the plate, preparing to take his stance. "Mike was better. But he's in New York for a couple of weeks and we needed a replacement."

"Maybe. But Nick's easier on the eyes," Somer said, pulling the mask down over her face and getting into catcher's position.

"What's that supposed to mean?" Trent asked stepping into the box.

Somer looked at him through the metal cage protecting her face and saw that the crease on his forehead had deepened as though her comment had confused him. "Nothing really. Just an observation."

"When did you start looking at the guys on the force?" Trent asked, preparing for the first pitch.

"Monday," Somer replied. *The first time I saw Nick*, she thought.

"Don't get any ideas. Daultry goes back to New York when Mike gets back."

Trent's words seem to bring a cold chill to the air. For the first time, she grasped the fact that Nick was only in Hillsborough temporarily. And it bothered her. It bothered her a lot.

"The only thing I'm thinking about is how to get you out," she lied. She squatted behind the plate and thumped the pocket of her catching glove with her free hand. "I know you can't lay off the high, hard ones, and in a minute, my pitcher is going to know, too," she said with a chuckle. She then flashed the pitcher the sign for a high fastball and settled in. "No batter, no batter," she chanted as the pitch came home.

But Trent was ready and sent the ball screaming between center and right field. Somer threw off her mask and watched the play unfold.

She thought Trent would stop at third base and settle for an easy triple, but as he rounded the bag, she could tell he had other plans. Full speed, he headed down the line right at her, intent on scoring an inside-the-park homerun.

She looked at her brother, the wide grin on his face telling her that the train was coming and she was on the tracks. "Oh no," she groaned, planting her feet and waiting for the relay throw from the second baseman. This was not going to be good.

Just as she readied herself for the hit, she saw Trent get knocked sideways and land in a heap on the infield grass. She easily fielded the ball thrown her way and walked to her brother. When she got there she was shocked to see Nick on the ground with him. Apparently Nick tackled Trent right before he ran into her. Somer smothered a laugh.

"What on earth happened?" she asked.

"I thought he was going to knock you into next

week and that you might get hurt," Nick said looking up at her from his back.

"I didn't need saving," she replied. "Trent tried to push me around as we were growing up. I learned early on to take his hits."

"Get off me," she heard her brother say.

Somer watched as Trent tried to untangle himself from Nick. "Don't bother," she instructed, tapping her brother on the head with the baseball just as he shoved Nick out of the way and got up from the ground. "You're out and we win!"

She extended her hand to Nick, still on the ground on his back. "Well, my hero, you're going to need a getaway car and I need some coffee. How about it?"

Nick looked at the angry faces of his teammates across the baseball diamond. "It doesn't look like I'd be welcome in the locker room right now, so why not."

## Chapter Seven

Nick sat at a table outside the local coffee bar with a cup of black coffee and waited for Somer to return. She'd said she would only be a minute, but it had been a lot longer. Her double-latte-mochachino-decaf-tsai-chi coffee or whatever it was she had ordered was either going to get hot or get cold by the time she got back.

He slouched back in the metal bistro chair and crossed his ankles. Around him people went about their usual business, and it amazed him how casual they all were. Nothing at all like urbanites who, by virtue of sheer numbers, had to be on the alert in a city where something was always happening around them. Not that he was complaining. Since being here, he had been able to relax more in a few weeks than he had in the past ten years.

And then there was Somer. She had exactly the opposite effect on him. There was no relaxing around her, nor did he want to.

He saw her coming toward him and enjoyed the view. His eyes did a quick scan of her as she approached. Slowly he drew his back away from the chair and sat up straight. She didn't rock her hips back and forth like a lot of women did, for attention. Instead Somer walked straight and tall, confident with long strides. He liked that.

When she sat opposite him, he noticed for the first time she was carrying a huge ice cream sundae.

"Lordy, I need this," she said, dragging her spoon through a river of chocolate and what had to be caramel before digging into the vanilla ice cream beneath. She popped a healthy spoonful into her mouth and closed her eyes. "An extra hour a day at the gym for a week, but worth it."

Nick looked at the mound in the dish in front of her. "Are you going to eat all of that?"

She handed him a spoon. "No, you're going to help."

Nick took it from her and helped himself to a healthy spoonful of his own. "I haven't had an ice cream sundae in years."

"Why not?" Somer asked, catching a melting drip with the tip of her spoon before it hit the tabletop. "In a city as big as New York, there has to be a place open all day and night."

"I suppose there is. I just don't have the kind of time necessary to find one."

"Take the time, Nick. It's important."

"I guess."

She popped another spoonful into her mouth. "In any case, I have to say, you surprised me today."

"How so?"

"Charging out and tackling Trent like that. You know you're going to be locker-room talk for quite a while, don't you?"

Nick tunneled into a mass of vanilla. "If it's anything like NYPD, I can only imagine."

Somer laughed. "But you'll always be my hero."

It was Nick's turn to laugh. "Some hero. Two out and I tackle the tying run, who then turns into the third out."

Somer shrugged and ate another spoonful of ice cream, watching as Nick did the same. It was beyond her why a long silver sundae spoon holding plain vanilla ice cream covered in chocolate sauce should enhance a man's masculinity, but somehow as Nick helped her finished the sundae, the spoon did just that. She dropped her gaze to the tabletop, feeling betrayed by two inanimate objects. She picked up her drink and sipped it slowly.

"What is that anyway?" Nick asked.

"A number four."

"I know that, but I can't imagine why anyone would take a perfectly good cup of coffee and then dilute it with a bunch of flavorings." He watched as she drank it. "How's it taste?"

"Curiosity getting you?"

"I just wonder if it's worth ten dollars."

She held it out to him. "Want a sip?"

He declined with a shake of his head. "Black, hot and strong. That's the only way to drink coffee."

Somer raised her eyebrows in response. *Hot and strong.* That could easily describe Nick, too. She leaned back in her chair, trying to gather her scattered thoughts. Nick was more than handsome, in a rugged way. She could easily be tempted into trying to find out what made him tick. But he would be going back to NYPD in a few weeks. From what she could tell about him already, there was no doubt he was dedicated to both the city and his job, and she was not into the "summer love" thing like in high school.

Pity, because he was becoming darn interesting on top of his obvious great looks.

"It wasn't just your tackling skills that surprised me," she said, satisfied she had done enough ogling for the day.

"Oh? How else?"

"You don't strike me as a cop who would take time out of an investigation for recreational purposes."

"Who says I'm taking time off?"

Somer looked at a smile that sent her heart skittering. She felt the heat crawl up into her face. On top of everything else, Nick was also a man entirely too confident. She'd take care of that.

"Unless there are two of you, someone is not following up on the lead I handed you. Didn't they teach you at the academy that the first forty eight hours are critical to an investigation?"

"That they did," he acknowledged. "But they also taught us that it is important to step back and look at the whole picture once in a while so as not to miss anything."

She reached for a napkin and he handed it to her. His fingers barely brushed her palm, but it sent a sensation up her arm. She was sure he could see it in her eyes.

"I'm having one of the patrol officers check to see if any cars were ticketed for black out glass in the last six months. I should have the report in a day or two."

"Great. And then we can check out anyone who has," Somer replied, anticipation in her voice.

"That is probably not a good idea."

She slid her elbows onto the tabletop and swirled the last bit of melting ice cream with her spoon. "Why not?"

Nick looked at her as she waited for his answer. There was an incredible naturalness to Somer. One he liked. He tried to think of one woman he knew in the city who would sit outside in plain view wearing a dirty baseball uniform stirring melting ice cream and couldn't come up with one name. The women he knew remained perfectly dressed and spotless no matter what the occasion. Now he could add perfectly boring to the equation.

"Because you're a civilian and getting involved in a police investigation is not a wise thing to do," he finally answered her.

"Unless the information you find needs someone with local knowledge to help you piece it together."

"That's what your brother is for."

"I got the mayor to cave, remember? My brother wouldn't know that the mayor doesn't handle pressure very well, but I do from talking to some of the stringers who cover local council meetings. The mayor is up for re-election this year and can be very skittish about adverse publicity." She waved her spoon in the air. "Scandal is not good for the campaign."

"I appreciate the tip, I really do. Still, police work is best left to the police."

Somer slouched back in the chair. "You can't stop me from following my reporter's radar, you know."

"I can arrest you if you get in the way, though."

"Try it," she challenged. "You're in my neck of the woods, Detective. I'm not without my contacts either."

"A lady on a mission," Nick suggested, and waited for her to respond to the baited statement. But Somer ignored it. "Okay, then, I have to tell you, you kind of surprise me, too."

"At the risk of taking a turn I may not like, how?"

"You're not seeing anyone right now. That's very surprising."

"How can you tell I'm not?"

"Because you spend too much time thinking about work, and no one was there to watch you play ball."

Somer furrowed her brow. "Quite a leap from locking me in a jail cell to asking for a date."

"I didn't ask you for a date."

"Then why the question?"

"I like you. You're different."

"Different good or different bad?"

He studied her for a while. "I'm not sure yet. But just to clarify a little, I do think that you are pretty."

"Well that's a relief. For a minute I was thinking Elephant Man different."

Nick shook his head. "You can cross that one off your list."

"To answer your question then, unfortunately, or fortunately if you ask my brother, I'm not interested in a relationship right now. I'm trying to concentrate on my reporting."

She knew that it used to be true at least. But since she met Nick, more than a passing thought about getting to know him better had filtered itself into her mind amid the deadlines and editor's marks. Unfortunately reality usually followed close behind and she knew Nick would be out of her life as fast as he'd entered. She'd have to be content to look and not touch while he was here.

"I can't imagine you not getting anything you wanted," Nick replied.

"I hope you're right because I don't want to just write for a regional paper forever."

"I thought you wanted to stay around here."

"I do, but I wouldn't mind being a correspondent and going on assignment, or maybe covering stories for one of the news services."

Admiration for her spirit made Nick smile. "Good, then you might be on your way to New York soon."

"Or LA or Washington." She smiled. "Or Paris or Rome."

"Well that would be a heck of a thing, wouldn't it?"

"What would be?"

"Your traveling all over the country or the world would get in the way of us."

"There is no us."

Nick held her mutinous look. "A potential us then." His own smile grew. "The moment I saw you rifling through my desk I think something happened."

"I wasn't . . . oh, never mind. Give it up, Daultry. You're going home soon to make New York streets safe and I'm going on to the ABC evening news." She dipped her head. "Reporters and cops, cops and reporters." She made a so-so gesture with her hand. "About as viable as oil and water."

Nick's smile turned into a grin. "And as interesting when they try to mix. Hey, maybe you'll get assigned to the city and I'll be just around the corner."

"You're impossible, Nick," Somer said.

"For the time being then, let me be your friend."

Warily, she sized him up. He was up to something, she just knew it. "Your friend?"

"Yes, try me out. We did get off on the wrong foot, but I'm not such a bad guy. My friends in the city would tell you that I'm a bit eccentric, but I'm not a jerk. I don't have many bad habits, well, I do tend to zone out during football season and don't get between me and the Giants, but for the most part I'm normal."

"Let's just see," she said laughing. "No promises, though."

Nick held out his hand. "Sounds like a plan."

Somer met it with hers. "Okay then."

Their fingers tangled and then, changing from handshake to hand holding, found the perfect fit. His gaze rose from their hands to her eyes as his thumb made lazy circles on the back of her hand.

"Your hand is soft," he said, still holding her with the intensity of his gaze. "Not at all like a catcher."

"It's the hand cream," Somer whispered, unable to tear her gaze from his eyes.

"I don't think so," Nick countered.

Somer felt a blush work its way up her neck and into her cheeks. Her pulse quickened, turning up the heat she felt inside her chest. It was ridiculous. It wasn't as though no other guy had ever looked at her like this before. It was just that she didn't want this particular guy to stop.

"Well, well, well," a voice from behind her said.

Instant recognition made her pull her hand free. "What are you doing here, Trent?" she asked when he came into full view.

"I should be asking you that," he answered. "Daultry," he said, acknowledging Nick. "Or should I call you something like," Trent clasped his hands together and fluttered his eyes in an exaggerated manner, "my hero." The rich sound of male laughter rose in response.

"You mean traitor," one of Trent's teammates corrected.

"Yeah, Daultry, we're trying to trade you as we speak," another said.

"Back to NYPD, that is," a third added.

There was more laughter accompanied by the slap of high fives. Nick accepted it all with a good-natured nod. "Sorry, you're stuck with me for at least another six weeks"

"We could go zero and ten in that stretch if your sister hangs around the field, Archer," someone shouted to Trent.

"I'll make sure she's too busy for that," Trent assured.

"If you don't I bet Daultry will."

There were more laughs and some typical male

comments that Trent allowed to go on until he was sure his sister and Nick were properly chastised. "Okay, that's enough guys," he finally said. "Why don't you head into Sara's and order me a burger before the kitchen closes."

With nods and questions about whose turn it was to buy, the guys filtered into the restaurant next to the coffee bar.

"So this is where you go after you throw a game," Trent said to Nick, sitting on an empty chair next to his sister. "And you," he said to her, "what did you promise him?"

"Nothing," she assured. She put her hand on Nick's shoulder. "The man is a bona fide knight in shining armor. You were about to clock me."

"I knew you could take it, sis," Trent replied. "I still have the scar from the time you knocked me into the trash cans during touch football last season." He turned to Nick. "A reporter who doesn't know the true meaning of the word 'touch.' Do you believe it?"

Nick's mind raced back to about ten minutes ago when, not only was he sure that Somer knew that meaning of the word, but had invented a whole new definition just by holding his hand. "I'm sure she didn't do it on purpose."

"Are you kidding?" Trent said rising, "my sister could stop one of the New York Giants heading for the end zone if she put her mind to it."

"So you're admitting then that you wouldn't have

scored on me without Nick's help." Somer said quickly.

"How do you do that?" Trent asked.

"Do what?"

"Turn things around on me like that?"

"You make it so easy, brother dear."

Trent threw up his hands. "I give up. Don't hang around her too long, she'll have you babbling in no time." He saluted his exit and disappeared into the restaurant to join his teammates.

"I suppose I should get going too," Somer said.

"Too bad. It was getting interesting before your brother showed up."

Somer nodded. "And that's exactly why it's time to leave."


Back in his apartment, Nick stared at the ceiling as late-night television droned in the background. Glancing at his watch, he saw it was two in the morning. He padded through the darkened house to the kitchen and yanked open the refrigerator door. He fumbled for the juice and drank it right from the carton.

"Somer Archer," he whispered, tossing the empty carton into the sink. "You may as well have come home with me because I can't get you out of my mind."

Since he met her, she seemed to fill all the empty spaces inside him. He couldn't help that he liked her beautiful blue eyes that looked like a bottomless ocean and filled him with a peace he hadn't felt in years. Or her blond hair that reminded him of thick honey. Maybe it was her laugh with its vivid tones that made him want to join her each time he heard it.

Looking out the window, he saw that his neighbor's house was dark and silent. At least someone was able to sleep. Rubbing his face, feeling the bristly growth of beard beneath his fingers, he wondered if Somer was feeling anything at all for him.

He really liked her. She was a woman who knew herself and wasn't afraid to let people see her as she was. There was so much life in her eyes that he wanted to experience it with her and see what would happen next. If only she'd give him a chance to do it.

But she was like sunlight; coming and going on her own terms and filling a room with warmth when she was there. And how do you catch a sunbeam?

Think, Daultry, he chided himself. You're a cop, good at solving mysteries, complex cases and even cryptograms in the local paper. Why can't you just figure out how to solve this puzzle too?

The challenge hung provocatively in front of him as he paced the kitchen. The black car. Tomorrow he'd know if the beat cop found out anything about it. Somer wasn't going to let that lead alone, so he probably would have to make sure she stayed safe by taking her along with him if NCIC spat out any pertinent information.

They'd spend some time together and she could get to know him. Maybe they'd do lunch. No, dinner. As a friend, not as a date. Somewhere nice, but not too expensive. He didn't want her to think he was showing off or anything.

A smile grew on Nick's face as he savored the plan. He never met a woman who wasn't impressed with being wined and dined. Wait! No wine. Maybe sparkling water. Something nonalcoholic so she wouldn't think he was trying to soften her up.

Then he'd send her flowers and a note the next day saying how much he enjoyed dinner and ask if they could do it again. He didn't know a woman yet who didn't say yes to dinner after getting flowers. He nodded. It was a good plan.

Satisfied, he headed back to bed. Now he could sleep.

## Chapter Eight

The knock on Somer's apartment door caught her with her hand in a jar of jellybeans. The breakfast of the busy. She dumped the candy on top of the new spiral notebook next to the jar.

Opening the door, her lips parted. "Nick." His name came out in a rush of air.

His arm was braced shoulder-height against the door jam. A white paper dangled from his finger-tips. She set her curiosity aside for a minute because he looked great. He had a white button-down shirt with the sleeves rolled up to the elbows and a pair of well worn jeans, their perfect fit emphasized by a cocked hip as he stood there.

"What are you doing here?" Her gaze went from the paper in his hand to his eyes. The flicker of amusement she saw there almost made her want to grab the paper from him and read it. But she'd play his game for a while and see what happened.

"I'm working," he said. "Can I come in?"

"Sure." She stepped aside. Intuitively she sensed something was up. His appearance was too casual for a day at the cop shop. She closed the door and watched him stop in the middle of her living room.

"Very nice," he said. "It's like walking into a southern plantation."

He looked from the bouquet of mixed flowers on top of a cherry sideboard at the far wall to the basket of dried rose petals on a Queen Ann lowboy in front of the couch. His gaze then seemed to study the light peach paint on the walls and the brown empire sofa with its carved roses in the cherry wood. He ran his hand over one of the crocheted doilies on the end tables that accented the southern flavor she had so carefully crafted.

He turned to face her. "I wouldn't have pegged a catcher as being a romantic."

"Don't expect me to pull down the drapes and make a gown like Miss Scarlett. I don't know nothing about sewing no clothes," she said in a forced southern drawl. "I go to the mall for that."

"You look just fine in what you're wearing," he replied.

Somer flushed. She felt the heat in his gaze as it moved down her body. "You said you were working," she reminded him. "Does it have anything to do with the paper you're dangling in front of me, waiting for me to ask what it is?"

"As a matter of fact, it does," he replied with a smug look on his face.

Somer grabbed it from his hand.

"That's more of what I expected."

Somer looked up from the paper only long enough to catch another flicker of amusement roll across his eyes. "I try not to disappoint."

"You haven't so far anyway," was his quick reply.

She held up a hand for him to not talk for a moment. "Says here a ticket was issued for over-tinting last month. New Jersey License 5S5-F5T."

"And it was issued to a car right here in Hillsborough."

She looked up. "That makes it easy. Let's go." She scooped up more jellybeans and grabbed her notebook, then ran out the front door. Nick was right behind her. "Will it offend your masculine pride if I drive this time?" she called back to him.

"It depends on why you want to."

She dared an honest response. "I want to get there today."

Nick stopped in his tracks. "Are you suggesting that I drive too slow?"

"Were you in the same car I was in last time we drove together? The blue thing that didn't go over thirty five downhill?" She waited for his response.

None came. "Of course if you feel threatened . . ." she continued, allowing the comment to hang there.

"I do not feel threatened. And just to prove it, you can drive my car." He held out the keys.

Somer saw right through it. No matter who drove, his car would not go any faster. "Let's take mine."

"You don't like my car either?" He looked really hurt now.

"We're wasting time, Daultry."

"But you just insulted my car."

"I apologize. I love your car. I really do. If anything happened to it while I was behind the wheel, I'd never forgive myself." She ripped open her driver's door. "Now get in."

"Very diplomatic," Nick acknowledged, watching her get in and buckle her seat beat.

"You never told me where we're going."

"That's because I wanted to make sure you weren't going to find a way to get there without me." He got in beside her and strapped in. "985 Stagecoach Way."

Somer turned the key in the ignition. "Okay then. Let's go."

To Nick's credit he didn't flinch when she took the first turn at forty miles an hour. He just tightened his seat belt.

Nor did he tell her to slow down when her speedometer inched up to sixty in a posted thirty five. He just whispered what sounded suspiciously like a prayer.

And he said nothing ten minutes later when they screeched to a halt in front of a small four-unit apartment house on the other side of town. He just reached across, grabbed the keys and tucked them into his shirt pocket.

Somer didn't waste time on becoming indignant about the gesture. She was out of the car and running to the back parking lot before Nick could work up a smirk. He appeared less convinced of the urgency, because he followed her at a leisurely pace.

Halfway to the back, she realized he was setting her up and slowed her pace. She turned and gave him a knowing smile. "The car's not here, is it?"

"Nope."

"You checked before you came over."

"Yep."

"Then why did you let me break about a dozen motor vehicle laws on the way over here?

"To see what you'd do."

Somer glared at him. "Okay, Daultry, apparently you have a plan. Let's hear it."

Nick pointed over her shoulder. "Do you know who lives here?"

"No . . ." She drew out the word.

"Sarah Carson. Single mom."

"Okay, so are you saying she drives the black Camaro with the tinted windows?" she asked with a touch of annoyance in her voice.

"No, but I think her teenaged son does."

"And you also think he had something to do with the bank robbery?"

"We won't know until we check out the kid and the car." He turned and began walking back to the street. "Let's hope that our driver went to school today."

After checking in with school administration, Nick and Somer waited in a parking slot across from the Camaro.

"Why don't we just ask the principal to call our boy down to the office?" Somer asked, watching the kids coming out of the building.

"This is much more fun. We wait until he comes out with his friends. In front of the 'establishment'," Nick skewed the word when he spoke it, "our guy might clam up. In front of his friends, he just might want to show off and reveal more than he would have otherwise. There," Nick pointed to a group of kids coming toward them. "I bet the guy in the middle is ours."

Somer's gaze followed Nick's direction. In the middle of a group of about five boys and girls, a tall dark-haired young man dressed in dark clothes had his arm looped around the shoulders of a skinny blond girl. She watched as he dug into his pocket and produced a set of keys. In a second the telltale beep and flash of lights on the Camaro pegged him as its owner. Nick was already out of the car and on his way by the time Somer opened her door.

"Your ride?" Nick asked the young man.

The boy had just put his hand on the door latch. He straightened and turned to the voice. "Who wants to know?"

Nick held up his ID. "Detective Nick Daultry. Can we talk for a minute?" The kids surrounding the boy began to disperse. "Tell your friends they can stay. This won't take long."

The kid nodded to his friends. They assumed various annoyed poses and waited.

"I didn't do nothing," the kid said.

"Are you James Carson?" A few of the kids started to snicker.

"Dakota," James corrected. "I don't go by James."

"Dakota, then," Nick said. He tapped the hood of the Camaro with his forefinger. "Yours?"

"Yeah, why?" James looked for scratches in the finish as he spoke.

Nick tapped a knuckle on the window. "Black out glass."

"So?"

"Against the law in New Jersey." Nick walked around the car as he spoke. He leaned down, cupped his hands on the back window and tried to look inside. "What do you have in there you don't want anyone to see?"

"Nothing," James said.

Nick straightened. "Show me."

James got in and started the car. The whine of the

electric windows followed. Nick leaned his forearms in the open window and scanned the interior. "Pretty nice. Looks like the navigation and Bose music systems are new." He looked down at the floor. "Neon floor lights. Sweet." The electric windows started to go back up and Nick had to back his arms out or get caught in the way. "You must have quite the part-time job to afford all that."

"What I got or ain't got is none of your business," James shot back.

"That's all pretty expensive stuff."

"So?"

"So your mom works two jobs just to keep you in new toys?"

James gripped the steering wheel with both hands. "You want something specific?" He looked at Somer. "Or you just showing off for your girlfriend there?"

She surged forward but Nick caught her by the arm. "Just asking," Nick replied.

James signaled to his friends to get in the car. As they brushed past Nick and Somer, James revved the engine. "I'm a minor. I don't have to talk to you without a parent present."

"Maybe not, but I can still give you a little advice," Nick replied in a calm, even tone. "Get the tint off the windows before you get picked up again or I'll have the car impounded until you do."

When the last door slammed shut, James stepped

on the gas and sped away. Nick and Somer watched as he fishtailed out of the parking lot.

"Great job, Kojak. Now he knows you're on to him," Somer said, shaking her head.

"Exactly. If the rural juvies are anything like the urban juvies, he's going to want to prove to his friends, and to me, that he wasn't intimidated in the least. He'll make some stupid, macho move and that, oh ye of little faith, is when he's going to screw up. And when he does. I'll be right there."

"You mean *we'll* be right there, don't you?" Somer corrected.

"I guess I'm going to have to get used to having you around."

"You got that right," Somer said firmly.

Nick looked at her. "If you're with me, you're only there to observe. There'll be no talking, no cross-examination, nothing."

She pressed a hand to her chest. "Did I say a word ten minutes ago when you were playing 'Law and Order'?"

"Somer, you haven't listened to me once since we met. I am not reassured by your sudden loss of words." He furrowed his brow. "By the way, why didn't you say anything?"

She shot him a sudden innocent smile that didn't seem to reassure him either. "While you were having so much fun being Joe Cop, I was busy observing his friends. I'd say by the body language, you made one or two of them a bit nervous. I heard the redhead call the kid in the varsity jacket 'Matt.' How about we go inside, look around, talk to a few kids and find out Matt who?"

Nick nodded, a smile growing on his lips. "Nice work. Tell you what. You go inside and see what you can find out, and I'll catch up to *Dakota,* follow him for a while, and see what shakes out."

She nodded and took two steps toward the building before turning back. "Just one thing."

"Yes."

"We do make a pretty good team, don't we?"

"Seems that we do." Nick walked to her and drew her into a hug.

Surprised, but pleased, she put her arms around him returning the favor. It was a nice hug. Reassuring. Maybe even slightly sexy. It made her feel good.

"Thanks, Daultry," She said when they parted. "You've just made this case really interesting."

"Glad to oblige," he said.

And she could tell from the look in his eyes that he meant it.

## *Chapter Nine*

Somer logged onto the Internet on her desktop at work and went to Google. She'd done some late night surfing on the web at home and wanted to recheck a few sites before she started on her assignment story for the paper. But instead of typing in 'resale markets' to check to see if any of the stolen merchandise from the B&Es were being offered for sale locally, she found herself typing in 'Nick Daultry.' It couldn't hurt to see what popped up, she reasoned.

"I hope you haven't made plans you can't break for Saturday night," the senior editor at the paper said.

Somer frowned and quickly minimized the screen. "Greg, I told you I'm not going to the awards banquet."

"Even if you're getting an award?"

"You can't know that."

He sat down at the chair next to her desk. "Oh but I do."

"The winners of the Regional Reporting Awards are the best kept secret in this place." She narrowed her eyes. "You're just trying to get me to go so I can meet your newly divorced brother, aren't you?"

"Families are invited and I am up for an award, too. He could be there."

"Nice try, but I'm not going."

"Yes, you are," Greg said, his face suddenly serious.

"Greg, what is this all about?"

"Mr. Biltwell, our illustrious owner, sent me to make sure that you'd be there. You're not getting a Regional Reporting Award, you're getting the Publishers Award for your story on the Angel of Mercy case, and he wants you there in person to accept it."

Somer looked at him for a moment and then laughed, the chuckle coming out more like a sniffle from her nose. "Yeah, right. I told you, I am not meeting your brother."

"I'm serious, Somer. Everybody knows you never go to the awards dinner, even when you got one four years ago. Well this time it's a big deal and you have to be there. Channel 12 New Jersey is coming to cover the presentation, and I hear that maybe one or two of the major New York networks might send a stringer to check it out. You can't embarrass Biltmore by not showing up."

Somer looked around the room. It seemed like everyone in earshot was waiting for her answer. What else could she do? Defy the überboss in front of everyone? Not when she was about to ask him for a raise.

She held up her hands. "Okay, I'll do it. But I'm only staying for the presentations and then I'm out of there."

A satisfied grin spead on Greg's face. "That's enough time for you to meet my brother, Leonard."

"Then he'll also be meeting my boyfriend," Somer quickly said without putting much thought into what she was doing.

Greg's face crinkled. "I didn't think you had one."

"We just started seeing each other recently."

Inside her head, Somer's sensible side was shouting *Stop! Don't say another word. You don't have a boyfriend.*

"So he'll be coming with you then?"

"Yes, he's very supportive of my career."

*Now you're going to have to get a boyfriend by Friday night*, the voice inside Somer's head reminded her. *And not only a boyfriend, a supportive boyfriend.*

"I must say I am surprised."

"How so?"

"I didn't think you had time for dating. You seemed so focused on your career lately."

"As I said, Nick is very supportive."

"Nick, huh? Well, at least we have a first name."

Somer felt her heartbeat rise. Holy faux pas, did she really say Nick?

Greg stood. "I guess I'll see you both on Friday." He shook his head. "Leonard will be so disappointed."

As Somer watched him leave, her mind was already spinning with how she was going to pull this all off. She slid her elbow onto her desk and rested her forehead in her hand. What had she done? Now she had to somehow explain to Nick that she needed a favor from him.

And not just any favor, a big favor, an I-need-a-boyfriend-so-I-can-avoid-a-fix-up-favor. A favor like that was normally reserved for best friends who knew each other for years.

As Somer maximized the search screen on the desktop, she briefly wondered if she should forget everything, just call Greg and confess the whole thing. After all, how bad could meeting a nuclear physicist named Leonard Wilkonstats possibly be?

Despite her predicament, there was one thing Somer thought she should check out on her own before facing Nick. Glad that some of Matt's friends at school were so eager to share information once she told them she was doing a story on the football team, she'd found out where he had an after-school job.

She hopped in her car and drove to the local big box hardware store. Grabbing a cart from the parking lot, she pushed it into the garden center and began walking up and down the aisles.

The big lawnmower sale had just ended, but there were still plenty of pink flamingos to be had. She scooped up two of them, stood them in her cart and looked around for a sales clerk. She found the one she wanted watering some plants.

"Excuse me," she said.

The young man whirled around and nearly soaked Somer with the hose. "Sorry," he said, clicking off the water.

"I didn't mean to scare you . . ." she peered at his nametag, "Matt. I'm looking for some shrubs to put in the front of my house."

"What kind?" Matt asked.

"Oh, something with flowers."

"There's some in the back."

"Have you worked here long?" Somer asked.

"About six months."

"Then maybe you can answer some questions I have?" He had no idea she didn't mean about horticulture.

Matt shrugged. "Sure."

Somer walked along side him as they headed for the back of the garden center. "It's good to see young people working. Not like some people." She saw Matt give her a sidelong glance. "I mean with the rash of break-ins these days, it seems like people would rather take things than earn them."

"I suppose." He stopped in front of a rhododendron. "My mom likes these. We have a lot in front of the house."

"They're nice," Somer replied. "Do they get tall? Because if they do, I wouldn't want to put them in. You shouldn't have tall shrubs near the house. That makes a perfect hiding place for someone trying to break in."

Matt shifted from foot to foot. "I don't know nothing about that."

"I mean," Somer continued noting that Matt's body language told her he'd rather be anywhere else but with her, "you can't be too careful these days. But I think the police have some good solid leads and are close to naming some suspects, so maybe some tall shrubs would be all right. One of the theories is that it's a bunch of kids. What do you think?"

Matt bit down on his lower lip and looked away. Somer waited, letting him alone with his thoughts, hoping he would offer some bit of information he didn't even know he might have.

"Do you think it would be safe for me to put in some of those shrubs? With the police close to breaking the case, I mean," she asked after a few moments.

She saw Matt flinch. "Why are you askin' me?"

Somer shrugged. "No reason. Just making conversation."

Matt was getting antsy. He was tapping his fingers against his thigh and wouldn't make eye contact with her. He knew something. She could just feel it. She had to refrain from shaking him until she found out what it was, but a teenager was not the kind of interview you rushed. He'd get all nervous and defensive if he thought she was getting too close.

"We done?" he asked.

"Yes, and you've been a great help."

After watching him leave, she turned the cart and made a left into the main store. Her thoughts drifted like tumbleweed in the wind as she headed for the service desk. Could she have accidentally stumbled on to something? Could the perps actually be kids? Did Matt really know more than he was willing to share?

A sales clerk behind the counter looked up as Somer approached customer service. She slipped her glasses off. "May I help you?"

"I'm hoping I can speak to someone in charge of personnel," Somer said.

"Why?"

The question caught Somer off guard. She had hoped to run into some young clerk like Matt; someone who wasn't too concerned with store rules.

"I'd like to get the address of that nice young man in the garden shop. He was so helpful."

"Which clerk?"

"A dark-haired young man. Matt, I think."

"That would be Matt Brown."

Somer knew that. She'd found that out at his school. "He told me his mother had some rhododendrons in the garden," she said in her sweetest voice, "and I wanted to ride by the house and take a look at them before I purchase some." What a lame excuse, she thought. The clerk is not going to buy any of it.

And she didn't. The sales clerk's mouth turned down into a frown of displeasure. "I'm afraid that won't be possible. Our personnel records are confidential and can only be accessed by written request and approval of management."

"How long could that take?"

"A week or more."

"That long?"

"Yes, now if you don't mind, I have work to do." The clerk put her glasses back on and returned to the computer keyboard. Somer clearly had been dismissed.

But there was still hope. Out of the corner of her eye, Somer saw two young girls punching in at the time clock. She waited until they hit the floor.

"Ladies," she called to them. "Maybe you can help me."

"Whatcha need?" the blond with the dark roots asked.

"I'm hoping you two know the sales clerks here."

"Only the hot ones," she replied with a giggle.

"How about the guy in the garden shop today, Matt Brown?"

The blond smiled, her expression becoming lively. "Everybody knows Matt."

"Do you know where he lives?"

"Wait, you aren't a stalker or anything, are you?" the other girl asked.

"No, he said his mother had a nice garden and I just wanted to see it before I bought some plants." Somer smiled, hoping to look sincere.

"He doesn't go to my school so I'm not sure exactly where he lives," the blond said, "but his father is the mayor of somewhere. Does that help?"

Somer smiled. "It sure does."

As she walked out of the store, she smacked her forehead with the heel of her hand. Matt Brown. Of course. The mayor's son. She knew that, so why hadn't she connected the dots?

She knew that too. Nick Daultry. She made a mental note not to let Nick distract her that much ever again.

## Chapter Ten

Linking all the small tidbits and facts she managed to collect from her trip to the garden center, Somer was sure she was on to something. With a little pressure laid on him, Mayor Brown had reluctantly let it slip that he saw a car with black out glass in the parking lot the day the bank had been robbed. A car with black out glass and tricked out well beyond what would be considered a normal teenager's means belonged to a young man who seemed to be tight with the mayor's son. The kid had to be getting the money for all the bells and whistles somewhere, and she didn't think his mom was giving it to him. And now there was a connection to the mayor's son.

Maybe separately not earth-shattering information,

but in thinking about the B&E's and following the leads, it posed some interesting theories.

Nick said he thought the robberies were sloppy; not done by professionals. What if it was some kids who were just bored and decided to liven things up a little around town? Not much had been taken from the homes; some laptops, iPods, DVDs, a few small televisions. Things easy to carry and easy to sell.

While she didn't think kids pulled the bank heist and it could be a stretch, with the mayor's son now tied to the owner of the black car, it could explain why the mayor was making the municipal deposit that day. Maybe the mayor knew more than he let on. Maybe his son was even involved directly with one or both cases. Maybe he was in the bank parking lot to try to make some sort of deal with the owner of the car and the bank robbery was an unfortunate coincidence for him.

And those possibilities would only make sense to someone familiar with small town politics. She knew how jumpy the mayor got with a bad story in the paper or some negative letters to the editor. If his own son was somehow involved in one or both cases, the mayor would do anything to try to make nice so there would be no headlines with his name in them.

Her mind spun with the possibilities and her reporter radar blipped. But she had more detective work to do before she could present her theory to Nick.

*Nick!*

Her full-of-herself enthusiasm had almost distracted her from the hole she had dug for herself. Almost, but not quite. It was no use putting it off much longer. This situation would be best dealt with quickly.

She found Nick at his desk reading the *Central Jersey Ledger.* "Reading my competition?"

He folded the paper closed. "You work for a major news service and this is a weekly tabloid. I don't think this is exactly your competition."

Somer snatched the paper from his hands. "That doesn't mean we reporters don't compete journalistically for every story."

"I didn't mean to insult your profession." Nick gave her an exaggerated bow of his head. "Your skills are beyond reproach."

"You can say that again. That's why I'm here."

"And I thought you were drawn to my charm."

Her lips twitched with amusement, but she let the comment go unchallenged. "Remember that you sent me back into the school to see what I could find out about the kid in the varsity jacket?"

"Don't tell me you got a date with the gym teacher?"

"No, I thought I'd let you do that."

Nick's eyes narrowed. "Very funny. Get to the point."

"I found out some interesting information." Somer walked around the office, aimlessly picking up and putting down objects like she wasn't dying to tell him. Although she thought she would burst, she'd let him suffer a little while longer for the competition remark. "Nice pen," she said, picking up a black Mont Blanc. "Yours?" She held it out to him.

Nick took it and stashed it in the top desk drawer. "I'm not going to ask," he said. "I can wait. You'll cave. It's obvious you need my help; otherwise you wouldn't be here."

"Nick, Nick, Nick," Somer said with an exaggerated sigh. "These are liberated times. Women can do all sorts of things without a man to help."

"You can teach me all about them later," he said. "I have no doubt that you are quite capable on your own."

"Flattery, Daultry? I'm stunned."

Nick grinned at her. "Is it working?"

"To a point."

"Then I'll have to try it more often."

"Okay, I'll tell you." She saw a satisfied smile grow on his lips. "Seems our football boy is the mayor's son."

Nick nodded. "Interesting, but not case-breaking."

Somer held up her hand. "Allow me to finish. I

went to the store where he worked and talked to him."

"Not a good idea, Somer."

"A very good idea," she refuted.

"Why? Did he confess?"

"Not exactly, but he seemed to get very nervous when I started talking about the police thinking kids were involved in the home invasions."

"The police don't think that. I do," Nick corrected.

"Technically you are the police even though you're just visiting, and when we establish a credible link between the robberies and the kids, the rest of the force will think so, too."

Nick's face told Somer he was interested. "By all means then, continue."

"I can't. Not yet."

Nick threw up his hands. "Somer, you are the most exasperating woman I have ever met. Do you know something or not?"

"I don't know anything for sure, but I have a hunch."

"I can't make a case on a hunch, Somer."

"But I can make a story." She began to talk like a steam valve letting go. "I don't think the two cases are connected. I think the mayor was just at the right place at the wrong time. And it's legendary around here how nervous he gets at election time. I think he carries a fire extinguisher in his pocket from September to November every time he's up for re-election to snuff out the proverbial fires."

Nick studied her face, but couldn't seem to figure out what she was trying to say. "But why would he give up the car so easily if his son was involved?"

"Only after we pressed him. Listen, I've lived here all my life. I know these people. Local politicians get all nervous talking to reporters about anything when they are running. They hate bad press. I bet I can get him to give us more with the right story."

"You have no facts to go on. Aren't you worried about being slapped with a defamation lawsuit?"

"I'm not quite ready to write it yet. When I talked to the mayor's son, I got a feeling he knows more than he's willing to say. I was about to go on over to his house and stake it out for a while." She bit down on her lower lip, considering if she should ask him for the very big favor before or after they checked out the mayor's house. Suddenly losing her courage, she decided after would be better. "I thought maybe you'd like to come along."

Nick seemed torn between frustration and curiosity. He settled for what he thought would be the middle ground. "Good thinking because you shouldn't be digging into this alone."

"You keep saying that. Nothing's going to happen to me."

"Things can go wrong, Somer, even with the most carefully crafted plans." Darkness settled onto his face, emphasizing the serious of his mood.

She wanted to ask him how he knew, but the look in his eyes told her not to do it. "Bear with me for a little while. I think Matt Brown is the key. All we have to do is watch him and see what develops over the next few days. I'm close, Nick, I can feel it."

"I just don't want you to get hurt, Somer."

"Daultry, I promise I'll do my very best not to inconvenience you by getting in the way or doing anything that might draw blood."

He apparently realized that he was fighting a losing battle because his eyes suddenly softened. "Good, because I have some plans for later that may just interest you."

"What kind of plans?"

"You'll just have to bear with me on that one."

As he spoke, his gaze roamed over her face. Her pulse skidded and jerked. When his gaze settled on her mouth, her mind became preoccupied wondering if his lips would feel as soft and warm on hers as she imagined they might. How she resisted the urge to trace his mouth with her fingertips, she didn't know.

She knew he was talking. She could see his lips moving but she didn't hear a word. Instead she concentrated on the way his cheeks dimpled as he spoke, the small dents adding interest to an already appealing face. When she looked closer, she could see the faint traces of the beginning of a five o'clock shadow near his jawbone. Was there anything more attractive than a man with a faint beard at the end of the day? At this moment, she didn't think so.

"Somer, you haven't heard a thing I've said," were the first clear words she finally heard him say.

"Nonsense, I hung on every word," she countered.

His forefinger did a quick circle in the air as if he wanted her to repeat it.

For a second she almost panicked and confessed that not one word had gotten through to her during her silly preoccupation with his mouth. But she refused to give him the satisfaction. She'd give it a shot at least.

"You said that you didn't want me to compromise the case by tipping your hand. If the kids got suspicious, you thought they'd dump the loot." It was probably what he said, she surmised as she whispered a silent prayer.

"Close enough," she heard him say.

"I don't suppose that since we kind of agree on what may be happening, you now realize that I'm not totally inept and can contribute to solving this case?" she asked.

"I never thought you were inept, just a little anxious."

"Listen, I'll make you a deal. If this stakeout doesn't pan out, I'll buy you dinner for wasting your time." She extended her hand. "Deal?"

He took it in both of his. "Deal. But I warn you, I can eat a lot when I'm hungry, so I don't come cheap."

The warmth of his grip and the look in his eyes made her not even care.

## *Chapter Eleven*

"Take this left," Somer said, directing Nick to the last street in town.

She looked from the open field beyond the municipal offices and the library on the outskirts of town to his profile. She found herself studying his jawline with renewed interest and his mouth with an all too familiar awareness. As much as she tried to deny it, Nick had carved a little place for himself inside her head. The more she saw him, the more her attraction to him grew. She liked a challenge, and Nick challenged her plenty. She knew she was up to the task and could give as good as she received. But from the way they always seemed to spar each time they were together, she didn't know what he thought about her.

"You never said much about my theory," she continued, unwilling to try to sort her feelings out at the moment.

"That the bank robbery and the break-ins are totally unrelated?"

"And that the mayor knows something."

Nick glanced at her and then turned his gaze back to the road. "It's a good premise," he admitted, "but I'd be happier with something concrete before I unleashed the dogs."

"What do you mean?"

Nick's gaze wandered back to her for another brief look. "If I present the idea to the chief, he'll have to call the county prosecutor. Once the prosecutor's office is involved, his detectives will be all over the kids and their families. It could be upsetting for the parents, especially if the whole thing turns into a dead end, and I'd like to have some kind of proof before that happens."

"Maybe we can find something at the mayor's house."

"Maybe." Nick lifted a hand from the steering wheel and pushed up the cuff of his sleeve to reveal a sportsman's watch. "It's four-fifteen. The kid should be at work and the mayor shouldn't be home yet. We may have some time to poke around a bit."

The simple gesture captivated Somer to the extent that they nearly drove by the house. "That's it,"

Somer said, recovering just in time. She pointed to the left. "The white house."

It seemed like Nick was out of the car the minute the engine stopped. "Stay here," he instructed. "Let me check it out first."

"Okay," Somer replied. No sense upsetting the man. She still needed to ask him to be her date for the awards dinner. She watched him walk to the front door and ring the bell. After a few moments, she saw him shrug and signal that he was going around back. She began to get out of the car when his second signal to her was an obvious 'stay put.' Reluctantly she nodded. As Nick walked down the long driveway next to the house, she saw him glance over his shoulder a few times to make sure she did.

Somer didn't know how long Nick expected her to wait, but she considered thirty seconds long enough and got out of the car. She had just started to walk toward the driveway when a car turned onto the street. Not sure if it was the mayor coming home, Somer did a quick about face and walked down the sidewalk away from the house. When the car continued past her and down the street, she turned and began walking back to the house.

Suddenly the street got busier. Another car came by and then another, making Somer turn first one way and then the other. Feeling more like an undercover passerby than a reporter on a story, she soon found herself pacing up and down the sidewalk with the precision of a guard at Buckingham Palace.

"This is ridiculous," she muttered, turning back toward the house. Just when she was about five feet from the house, the black car James drove turned onto the street and slowed as it approached the mayor's house. She thought it was going to turn into the driveway when suddenly the driver gunned the engine and sped off, tires squealing.

Another car approached and, this time, turned into the driveway. It stopped at the mailbox and the driver reached out the open window to retrieve some envelopes and the evening paper.

What else could go wrong, Somer thought. She concentrated very hard on getting an ESP message to Nick. She didn't know exactly what he was doing in the back of the house, but she did know that one of the occupants was home and he was about to get caught. Unfortunately, he didn't seem all that responsive to ESP because a minute later he came walking down the driveway.

The occupant of the car got out. It was the mayor's wife. "Who are you?" Somer heard her demand.

"Nick Daultry," he replied.

Closer now, Somer could see his disarming smile. She was impressed. For a man who came here intent on breaking a case, he had switched gears quite nicely. He apparently was a little intuitive because his intense cop demeanor had vanished, replaced by a more casual manner. She'd have to compliment him on that later.

"I'm with her," he continued.

The lift of Nick's brows hinted to Somer that he was expecting some help. Glad she had never officially met the mayor's wife, she walked to the woman and extended her hand. "Hi, I was just admiring your rhododendrons." She saw the woman glance to the plants. "I was at the garden center earlier. I'm thinking about putting some in my garden. Your son, Matt, told me that I could come down and take a look your landscaping. You must be his mother."

Reluctantly the women shook Somer's hand. "Yes. And you are?"

"They are beautiful," Somer said, carefully avoiding using her name. "Are they hard to care for?"

"They can be," Matt's mother replied, her brows furrowed telling Somer that she was still a bit confused by their appearance at her home. She looked at Nick. "There are none in the back."

Somer spoke up quickly. "I think I'll a buy a few."

"Yes, we should. And now would be a good time," Nick said.

"In a moment. What do you feed them?" Somer asked.

"We really should leave, dear," Nick said, his

tone underscoring that she shouldn't argue with him. "Little Johnny will be home from soccer practice soon. You know how he hates to come home to an empty house." He walked to Somer and put his arm around her shoulders. "And then there's the matter of dinner."

Somer nodded. It appeared that dinner was going to be on her after all. "Yes, honey. You don't have to remind me how hungry you get when things don't go your way."

Nick noticed another car approaching. He took Somer's arm and guided her to the car. "Sorry to disturb you," he said, opening the car and practically stuffing Somer inside. "We'll let you know how we make out with the flowers. Have a pleasant evening." Then flooring it, he drove off like a stock car racer.

"That didn't go very well," Somer noted, adjusting her seatbelt.

"Good Lord, Somer. You were supposed to wait in the car, not call attention to yourself."

"Me?" Somer feigned surprise. "What about you? I thought we were undercover. You practically gave her your life's story. Well, not your life's story, but somebody's. Exactly what time do we have to pick up little Johnny from soccer practice?"

Nick looked over at her. "You sound annoyed."

Somer glowered back. "That's unfortunate because I meant to sound angry."

"What about you? All of a sudden you're the green gardener or something. What did you think you were doing anyway?"

"Investigating, if you had let me finish," she retorted. "I would have gotten some information that may have tied everything together."

"How do you know that?"

"Because I'm good," she said quickly. "And I'm cute. You said so, remember?"

The remark caught Nick off guard and he almost laughed, but controlled it. "What does cute have to do with it?"

"People like cute. It makes them comfortable and opens them up. Didn't they teach you that in police school?"

"Not quite."

"Then watch 'CSI.' Cute works every time."

Nick held a hand in a surrender gesture. "Okay. It's all my fault we didn't break the case tonight and I'm sorry as heck for worrying about you."

"I don't know what you're getting so huffy about. You agreed my theory was plausible and even agreed to come here with me."

"Obviously a lapse of judgment on my part."

Somer lifted one delicate eyebrow disdainfully. "Perhaps we should change the subject. Did you find anything in the back yard?"

Nick nodded. "A shed with a very big padlock."

"Did you get a look inside?"

"No. I heard the car and thought it would be a good idea not to be caught breaking in."

Somer looked over her shoulder. "Maybe we should sneak back there and see what's inside."

"I think we've called enough attention to ourselves for one night. Right now I'm hungry and you owe me dinner, remember?" He stopped at the intersection. "Which way to a really good restaurant?"

Somer sighed and pointed. "Right. Maggie's is right down the street."

Maggie's, also known as Mag's Bags because of the takeout business it did, was in a strip mall that lined a busy country road. It was a place that didn't do a lot of sit-down business and that's why Somer suggested it. She still had the little matter of the awards dinner. Maggie's would give her the privacy she needed to ask Nick to go but also the busy foot traffic she wanted in case he flipped out when she did.

"Turkey sandwiches, some macaroni salad, sweet pickles and iced tea. Not a gourmet dinner, but not bad," Nick said.

Somer slid the order onto the table and sat across from him. "I figured you had gourmet in New York and that country is what you needed tonight."

"I have to admit," Nick said, pouring the iced tea

into two plastic cups filled with ice, "you are giving me a lot to think about."

Taking a cup from his hand, Somer held his sincere gaze. "Is that a compliment?"

Nick nodded. "The more I think about the B and Es, the more I think you may just be right." He raised his cup. "To a lady who can show a veteran cop a few new angles."

Somer smiled. "Thanks."

She sipped her drink and looked at Nick over the rim of the cup. She found her gaze slowly roaming over his handsome face. From the curl that fell over his forehead and skimmed his eyebrows to the little scar she found on his chin, Nick had to be one of most attractive men she had ever met. For an instant, an image of him in a tux teased her mind before she remembered she still hadn't asked him to be her date, her boyfriend-type date.

Rolling her eyes, she decided to keep it light for the time being. "I bet that your girlfriend in New York wouldn't like a dinner date like this."

A smile grew on his lips. "What makes you think I have girlfriends?"

Her eyes narrowed. "You have more than one?"

He smiled broader, a rich laugh escaping his throat. "No."

"You have one then."

"I have none," he corrected. "At the moment."

Somer's shoulders relaxed. "Good." Her eyes widened when she realized she sounded much too happy about it. "I mean, it's good that you play the field. I firmly believe that men should not be rushed into anything, but how do you feel about fix-ups?"

Nick's face clouded. "You want to fix me up with someone?"

"Not exactly." She shifted in her seat. "Well, that's not entirely true. I do have someone in mind."

"You want me to go on a blind date?"

Somer grimaced. "Not blind exactly."

"But you do want me to go on a date?"

Somer nodded. "Yes."

Nick shook his head. "No."

"It's really important."

He shook his head again. "No, Somer."

"But it's with me." The words were out before her brain fully engaged.

"You? You're asking me out on a date?"

For some reason all she could do was clamp her teeth together and smile. Any words that tried to form were stuck in her brain revolving around the fact she hadn't done this very well.

Nick leaned forward and snapped his fingers in front of her eyes. "Earth to Somer."

She gave her head a tiny shake and blinked. She pressed her fingers to her forehead. "Wow, head rush. Give me a minute."

"I have a better idea," Nick said. "Why don't you

just tell me what's going on?" He finished what was left of his sandwich and waited.

Somer took a deep breath. "I need a date for Saturday night."

Nick's face showed surprise. "Really?"

"I'm getting an award for my story on the Angel of Mercy and I got myself into a jam. My editor's brother just got a divorce and he's trying to get me to go out with him. I don't want to, so I told my editor I had a boyfriend."

"And you want me to play him."

Somer nodded. "I did kind of say that his name was Nick, so it would make it easier if you did."

"Somer . . ." His voice was thick and trailed off uncertainly. An emotion that had nothing to do with police work flared in his eyes.

Just as the muscles inside her tightened in anticipation, she realized he had started talking again.

"I'll do it."

"You will? That's great!"

"But you owe me."

"Okay."

"Maybe you shouldn't agree so soon."

"You just saved me from having to spend the evening with a nuclear physicist and I didn't pay that much attention in science class, so, okay, I owe you."

She didn't know whether she was happy that he'd solved her date situation or that she'd actually be spending some quality time with him talking about something other than the town's juvenile problem. She didn't care which. She was going to see him in a tux and that was worth the humiliation she just endured.

"It's black tie, so you'll have to rent a tux," Somer added, casually finishing her sandwich.

"No biggie. I've done black tie before."

"Good," she said, standing. She gathered up the remnants of their dinner and placed them in the trash. "On the way home I'll give you the condensed version of what you need to know if we really were dating."

"I got it. You like reality TV and science fiction novels," Nick said, as he pulled up next to the curb at the townhouse. "Your mother's name is Tess, your father died five years ago and you have a younger sister named Ali."

"Good enough," Somer replied. "You can wing anything else that might come up as needed. After all, we've just started dating."

"Since we've been spending a lot of time together lately, I suppose I can handle that part of the plot."

The teasing glint that rose in his eyes made Somer's heartbeat rise just enough to whip some pink into her cheeks.

"Is the rest of your family going to be at the dinner?" he asked.

A cold chill ran down Somer's spine. She'd almost forgotten about them. "I don't think so," she said. "They're busy that day."

"Everyone?"

She nodded. "Yes. Mom's off on one of her charity jaunts and Ali has the Greenpeace thing." She hoped he didn't notice that her remark lacked sincerity.

"What about Trent?"

Somer waved her hand in the air and rolled her eyes. "He's probably working. He's always busy. It'll be just you and me."

He turned off the ignition. "That'll be nice," he said.

He smiled and, for Somer, everything else around them seemed to fade to a blurry background. The way he twisted his body in the seat to face her, one hand on the steering wheel, the other on the automatic shift between their knees, made the buttons on his shirt strain against the fabric. How she resisted the urge to pop one or two of them open, she did not know.

Something tight and restricting gripped her chest, while a weightless sense of expectancy buoyed her stomach. His hand came up from the gearshift slowly and, then, as if waiting for her permission, his fingers stopped, barely touching her cheek before moving again to tuck a stray lock of hair behind her ear.

"If I did have a girlfriend, I'd want one like you," he said as his gaze traveled slowly across her face to her lips before settling on her eyes. "Someone smart, confident, sure of herself."

"And cute," Somer said, her gaze falling to his lips. "Don't forget cute." She lifted her gaze from his mouth to meet his eyes, her lips falling open slightly. He smiled, his dimples forming two perfect hollows on a face she thought was absolutely perfect.

"Not cute, beautiful."

With a smooth, commanding movement, he slipped one arm around her shoulders, the other to her ribs, and pulled her close. He dipped his head and kissed her with a soft exploratory pressure that was filled with restraint. His lips were hard, warm and asked for no more than she was willing to give him. The kiss seemed to last forever and she pressed her hand against his chest more in surprise than anything else. Just before he pulled back, his lips parted to bestow a deeper, more intimate kiss at the seam of her lips.

Somer let out a breath of air that sounded more like a sigh. "Wow. Not that I'm complaining, but what was that about?"

Nick laughed at the look of surprise on her face. "I just thought that if we are going to be a couple, I should probably know how you kiss. In case someone asks."

Somer took a deep breath to shake off the feeling of the smooth, silky firmness of his mouth. Her chin tilted sideways. "I suppose my editor's brother might want to know for scientific reasons."

A smile broke out across Nick's face. "Of course."

"So how'd I do?"

"Not bad for a country girl."

Somer responded with a high short laugh. "Daultry, you are full of surprises tonight."

The smile died as he traced her cheek with his fingertip. "The guys at the station call me Daultry. My family calls me Nicholas. I want you to say my name, Somer."

"Why?" she whispered.

"Because I'd love to hear you say it." His throaty tone told her that the kiss had affected him more than he thought it would.

"Nick," she said in a soft voice as she struggled for composure and the return of a calm heart. She saw him close his eyes and let the word envelope him. Beneath her hand, still on his chest, she could feel his heart thudding.

Nick shook his head slowly. "I don't know what it is, but when I'm with you, I feel at peace." Then he winked. "When you aren't sparring with me, that is."

"Is that why you really kissed me?"

Nick leaned back but kept his arm around her shoulder. "You looked like you wanted to be kissed."

"Did I?"

His left hand moved. Its forefinger curled, then pressed lightly beneath her chin until she was forced to tip it up. For a moment his eyes stared into hers. "Yes you did, and I was glad to oblige."

Though she thoroughly enjoyed the kiss, she didn't want him to think that the invitation to the awards dinner came with an invitation for something more afterward. "Maybe it was the closeness of the confined space in your car," she said. She pressed her palm firmly against his chest and eased away. Though he released her, his shoulder still curved in her direction.

His eyes darkened thoughtfully. He reached out and touched the hollow beneath her lower lip with his thumb. Slightly rough on her skin, it sent a shiver up her spine. Then his hand fell away and he straightened in his seat.

"I'm sorry if I gave you the wrong idea." He gestured to her car. "Luckily you can get away fast."

It was only then that she realized they were back at the station rather than at her house.

"Almost forgot about my car. Thanks for the ride back." She started to get out but turned back to him. "And thanks for the save for award's night."

He reached out and traced the curve of her jaw. "I think it could be fun."

Somer smiled. "I'm glad you think that way."

"I find that I think that way a lot when I think

about you. In fact, there are times I can't get you out of my mind."

Two tiny lines appeared across Somer's forehead as she contemplated what he said. "Pardon me if I seem a little confused. You can't get me out of your mind, but you're letting me go home alone. Is that how they do it in the city?"

Nick lifted an eyebrow. "Who said I'm letting you go home alone?"

Her eyes narrowed. "But . . ."

"I think that I should follow you so I have my car to drive myself back to my place later, after I get to know my 'girlfriend' a little better. We only have two days to become the perfect couple, remember?"

Surprised by Nick's casual approach, Somer could only nod.

"And that's how we do it in the city," he added with a wink.

Somer felt irritation rise and then flee, replaced by something better, something exciting. "Just don't get lost following me home, Daultry."

"Nick," he emphasized in a soft voice.

"Nick," she repeated just as softly.

He searched her eyes and then nodded in satisfaction. "I'll see you in a few minutes."

As she got in her car and started it, her heart leapt to her throat. All the way home she was aware of Nick's headlights shining in her rearview mirror.

Her nerves hummed with anticipation and only once on the way back to her place did she have second thoughts about spending some private time with him.

At her townhouse, she parked her car in the driveway and Nick pulled behind it. Then he opened her door and drew her out and into his arms. In his embrace, she found she couldn't think at all.

"I think I'm going to like being your boyfriend, Somer," he whispered as his lips found a tender spot near her ear.

"But you're not and there's still time to change your mind if you feel uncomfortable with the pretense," she said softly.

"I think it's too late for that."

"Do I hear a note of regret in your voice?"

His lips curved into a faint smile at her perceptiveness. "It's nothing for you to worry about. I told you I'd help you out of this jam, and I will." His lips hovered above hers, not touching, but waiting.

"Okay then," she agreed and before he could start worrying about the implication of what he had agreed to do or the future or regrets, she stood on tiptoes and touched her mouth to his. She sought the warmth that would carry them beyond hesitation, warmth that would turn the pretense into reality.

She found what she was looking for in a breath-stealing kiss. For a man who was by-the-book in his professional life, Nick was amazingly adept in the nuances of kissing, capable of gentle subtlety and then fiery passion.

"Necking in front of the neighbors isn't what I had in mind," she whispered.

"I know," Nick agreed. Eyes never leaving hers, he brushed her hair away from her damp brow.

"I'd still like you to come in for a while," Somer said.

"I'd like that, too," Nick admitted. "And I promise I'll be a perfect gentleman for the rest of the evening."

Somer nodded. Only when her pulse slowed and sensibility returned to her mind did she put the key in the lock and open the door. "I recorded 'Survivor.' We can watch that."

"Nothing like watching a group of people trying to sleep in the rain to change the mood," Nick said following her inside.

"Sit anywhere," she said tossing her keys onto the table near the door. "I'll get us something to drink."

In the kitchen she put her hands on the counter and closed her eyes. What was happening to her? As quietly as possible she walked to the doorway and peered into the living room. Nick sat on the far end of the couch, his arm draped across the back, his hand tapping nervously on his knee.

She knew what he was feeling. She was feeling it,

too. This was insane. She could not possibly be falling . . . She stopped, refusing to put a name to it. She closed her eyes and reminded herself once again that it was too soon; this was not supposed to be happening. To her. To him. To them.

But it had.

## Chapter Twelve

Nick sat behind the desk at the police station, the phone receiver cradled between his shoulder and his ear. "Yes, a dozen roses," he said, taking the receiver in his hand. "I don't know. How many colors do they come in?" He pulled out the bottom desk drawer, leaned back in the chair and propped his foot on the hanging file folder frame inside. "Red. Make them red."

Nick listened as the clerk on the other end repeated the delivery address and then asked a question that made Nick pause. What did he want on the card?

"Let me think for a minute," he said.

He stared at the ceiling and did just that. To him being with Somer felt like what he thought running a car into a bridge must feel like; sudden, intense and uncontrollable. She drove him crazy with her theories, good as the last one was, and the way she threw caution to the wind and went after what she wanted.

A woman had never affected him this suddenly and this strongly. He'd had more than his fair share of girlfriends, beginning in third grade when he kissed Katie Hudson by the sliding board and told her that he was going to marry her. But Katie married someone else and almost thirty years later that was the closest he'd been to a serious relationship.

But now.

Last night after the kiss in the parking lot, all he and Somer did was watch "Survivor." They laughed, channel surfed during commercials, caught a few hockey scores on ESPN and bet lunch on who was going to get kicked out of the tribe. Who would have thought watching eight people stranded on a desert island eating tree bark would be so enjoyable?

*That's it!*

"On the card, put: *I never knew watching eight people eat tree bark could be so much fun. Nick.*" He straightened in the chair. "Read that back." He wanted to make sure the clerk got every word. Satisfied, he read off his debit card number and finished the transaction. Maybe he hadn't bought Somer dinner like in his plan, but he was still sure there was another date in his future. And he hoped it wouldn't be from just sending her roses.

He'd just hung up when Trent came in to work.

"Hey," Nick called to him. "Where's a good place to rent a tuxedo on short notice?"

Trent poured himself a cup of coffee from the pot one of the dispatchers had put on. "Why?"

"I'm going to that awards dinner and Somer said it was black tie."

"What dinner?" Trent asked leaning against the file cabinet.

"The one on Saturday. Somer said you had something to do and couldn't make it. Too bad you'll miss her get some sort of award."

Trent took a large swig of coffee before speaking. "This Saturday?" he asked, putting the cup down on top of the cabinet. "It's this Saturday?" He tapped the heel of his palm to his forehead. "Silly me. I thought it was *next* Saturday. Of course I'll be there. Just remind me where and what time."

"She said it was at the Bridgewater Manor. Cocktail reception at seven, dinner and awards at eight."

"That's right," Trent said. "So she asked you to take her?"

Nick nodded. "Said something about her boss wanting to fix her up with his brother. Somer told him she was already seeing someone and asked me to get her out of the jam."

"Oh," Trent said, drawing out the word. "You're her cover, so to speak."

"Are you okay with that?"

"Sure," Trent said, blowing out a short breath for

emphasis. "I'll be happy to play along with this one, but do me a favor, will you?"

"What's that?" Nick asked.

"Don't tell Somer I'm coming. I want to surprise her."

Nick's cop radar went on high. "You're not setting me up for some brother-sister thing, are you?"

Trent raised his hands in a don't-shoot gesture. "You? Never. Somer thinks no one will be there to help her celebrate. Our family does this all the time, so she may even be expecting one or two of us to show up. I just want to see the look on Somer's face when we're all there with her."

"All there?"

"Me, Ali, mom. We all love surprising Somer. So keep it on the down-low for one day and don't ruin it for her."

Nick closed the bottom desk drawer and stood. "Sounds fair. I guess I'll meet the rest of the family tomorrow night then."

A smile broke across Trent's face. "Oh you bet you will." He waited for Nick to leave the station before grabbing the telephone. "Mom," he said when Tess picked up. "What are you and Ali doing Saturday night?"

Somer paid attention to detail as she did her makeup in preparation for the awards dinner. She used the end of a cotton swab to remove a dark spot of eye shadow from beneath her lower lashes. It had been years since she cared enough to try to get everything perfect. Usually just some mascara and lipstick was enough, but today she wanted to look as though she'd stepped out of a fashion magazine. Today, instead of her usual fifteen minutes, it had taken her the better part of two hours to get ready.

And it was all Nick's fault.

Men were lucky, she mused. They did not have the ritual women had. A shower, a comb and some cologne was all a man needed, and he was ready to go.

She thought about what Nick's routine might be. A steamy shower would set the clean, fresh scent of soap onto his skin. A few dabs of maybe a musk-scented aftershave would probably also linger on his face and throat. He didn't need anything to accent his beautiful face except maybe a dab of men's hair gel to keep that unruly curl from falling across his forehead. But even if it did, she'd have an excuse to reach up and brush it back into place.

The eagerness for him to show up on her doorstep grew. *Am I that lonely?* she asked herself in response to the feeling. *No*, she decided, *not lonely in general, just lonely for him.*


Saturday evening Nick arrived at Somer's townhouse precisely at seven. As he walked to her front door, he put a finger between his neck and the collar of the tuxedo shirt and pulled it forward a little. He actually hated formal dinners and parties, but made an exception for this one.

Hand in a loose fist, his knuckles barely touched the door when he knocked. Though he was happy he'd be accompanying Somer to the dinner tonight, the last twenty four hours had given him time to think. And thinking led him to the conclusion that he didn't want to play at being her boyfriend. He'd much rather have the job for real.

Now all he had to do was convince Somer to give him a chance to prove it.

Before another thought could cross his mind, the door opened and she was there in front of him. Her hair was swept upward, fastened with a barrette that glistened like diamonds, her feathery bangs barely brushing her arched eyebrows. At her throat was a crystal pendant that caught the light.

The black dress she wore hugged her curves to perfection, its neckline tastefully celebrating her femininity. The dress ended a little above the knee to show just enough of her legs to make it interesting.

"God, you look beautiful," he managed to say. She turned in a slow circle to give him the full look, not realizing the captivating picture of seduction she made as she did. The fabric of her dress moved across her hips and around her legs just enough to tantalize even the most honorable of men. He began to hope this dinner came with music and dancing so he had an excuse to hold her in his arms.

She looked him over head to toe. "You don't look so bad yourself."

He stepped back. "I guess I do clean up rather nicely."

"Can't argue with you there."

"Thanks for the roses." Somer motioned to them. "You didn't have to do that."

"I wanted to."

His dimples were still present from the smile that accompanied his admission when Somer's eyes rose to meet his. "Well, they're beautiful."

The obvious return compliment caught in Nick's throat. He didn't want to sound phony. He'd have another chance to tell her how beautiful she looked before the evening was over.

"What's the plan?" he said instead.

Somer reached inside and grabbed her evening bag from the table near the door. "The plan is we go there, eat dinner, accept the award and leave, hopefully without people asking too many questions."

An odd feeling of disappointment filled Nick. "You don't think I can pull off this boyfriend thing?"

"It's not that," Somer replied, handing Nick her shawl and turning so he could slip it over her shoulders. "I'm not very good at games like this. I don't like to deceive people and tonight I have to con a full room."

Was this his chance? "Maybe we don't have to

con anyone," he said not knowing what he was going to do if she asked what he meant by that.

"Of course we do," Somer replied, locking the door and turning back to him. "If not, I'll have to meet the rocket scientist."

"Maybe he's a nice guy."

"I'm sure he is and I'm also sure there is a wonderful lab technician out there just waiting for him. I shouldn't get in the way of that. Their offspring could discover the cure for every disease on earth. Do you want me to stand in the way of that?"

"If you put it that way, I suppose not."

"I didn't think so." Somer took a deep breath and held out her hand. "Show time, Daultry."

He took her hand. "Let's do it," he said, walking her to his car.

He opened the passenger door and let her get in before closing it and jogging around the front to get in on his side. Right before he opened the door, he stopped

"Nick," he said in a voice so soft he was sure she didn't hear him. "I wish you would call me Nick."

## Chapter Thirteen

"Somer, thank God you're here. Greg's been looking all over for you," said Eva, one of the stringers at the paper. She met them in the parking lot of the Bridgewater Manor.

"I told him I'd be here," Somer replied as Nick gave the keys to his car to the valet.

"We've all heard that before. Classified even has a pool that's up to about thirty bucks already."

Somer walked with Eva into the building. "What kind of pool?"

"A when-you'll-show-up slash if-you'll-show-up pool." Eva looked at her watch. "Seven fifteen. I lost."

"Sorry to disappoint," Somer replied just as Nick joined them in the foyer.

Eva eyed him from head to toe. "Not so fast. Maybe you haven't."

The covetous look in Eva's eyes bothered Somer, but she had a role to play. "Eva, this is Nick. Nick Daultry, my date. Nick, this is Eva. She works with me at the paper."

"My pleasure," Eva said, extending her hand for Nick to take, but acknowledging Somer's marking of her territory with a look of disappointment. "If it doesn't work out between you two, I could be persuaded to help you forget her."

Nick laughed. "It's nice to know I have a falback position."

Feeling oddly possessive, Somer took hold of Nick's hand as soon as he released Eva's. "We should find out where we're sitting."

"Table two, but Nick will have to go it alone for a few minutes," Eva said, already steering Somer away from Nick. "Greg wants to go over the program with you."

As Somer broke contact with Nick, she felt as though he took the warmth with him. It was a feeling she didn't like one bit. "I'll catch up to you there," she said to Nick. "It's probably a table full of people from sales. Greg would do that to punish me. I'll get there as fast as I can."

"It's okay," Nick reassured. "I'll be happy to meet your friends and coworkers."

"If one's named Leonard, you and I are practically engaged," she called as Nick entered the dining room.

"Table two," Nick said holding his dinner card out to the two women already seated. "I hope I can join you."

"A handsome man like you, anytime!" the older of the two said as a twinkle lit her eyes. She extended her hand across the low multicolored centerpiece. "I'm Tess. Tess Archer."

"You must be related to Somer."

"I'm her mother," Tess replied, "and this is Ali, her sister." Ali nodded what appeared to be a disinterested acknowledgment.

"Nick, Nick Daultry."

"You know Somer?" Tess asked.

Nick's answer was cut by the sound of chair legs scraping against the floor as another man joined the table. "Is this table two?" the man asked, reaching over and turning the placard toward him. "Yes it is," he said, satisfied only when he saw the number in black and white, "I'm here."

"And you are?" Tess asked politely.

"Leonard. Leonard Wilkonstats," he said snapping out the napkin and putting it on his lap. "I'm Greg Wilkonstats's brother."

As Tess and Ali acknowledged Leonard, Nick sat back and scanned his competition. So this was Leonard, the guy Somer was trying to avoid. Short dark hair, black glasses, slight with a build that looked like the most exercise he got was sharpening pencils for the SAT's in which he probably got a sixteen hundred. He seemed harmless enough but Nick wasn't going to take any chances. He'd play his part well.

After exchanging pleasantries with Leonard, Tess turned back to Nick, who had taken the empty seat on her right. "You were about to tell me how you knew Somer," she said, sliding her elbow onto the table and propping her chin on her knuckles.

"We're dating," Nick replied, glancing at Leonard.

Tess sat straight up. "You are?"

"Since when?" Ali asked, looking a lot more interested. Even Leonard seemed to be paying more attention now.

"Since about a week and a half ago," Nick replied, smiling.

"Somer didn't say anything to me about meeting someone," Ali said. "Did she say anything to you, Mom?"

"Why no, she didn't. But I can't wait to find out more about this," Tess said in a tone that sounded more playful than curious. "How did you meet her?"

Nick's answer was cut off by Trent joining them. "Good, we're all here," he said, sliding out an empty chair. "I can't wait to see Somer." He looked around the room. "Where is she anyway?"

"She had to meet her editor and find out about the program," Nick replied. "She said she'd meet me at the table."

Trent rubbed his palms together. "Can't wait."

Nick's cop radar started blipping again. "Trent, what's going on here?"

"Nothing. I just love to surprise my sister. Goes way back to our childhood. Nothing for you to worry about."

"Never mind that," Tess said, sliding her chair closer to Nick's. "You were about to tell me how you met Somer."

Ali leaned forward to look at him around her mother. "Yes, do tell us all."

Nick looked around the table from face to face. Trent seemed much too happy, Tess was positively beaming, and Ali looked like the cat that had just eaten the canary. Even Leonard was listening.

He had no idea what story was about to fall out of his mouth, but he knew he would have to make it good.


This was crazy, Somer thought as she snaked through the tables in the ballroom making her way to table two. There was no earthly reason why she should she be wondering what Nick would think when he caught sight of her coming toward him, but that's exactly what she was doing. They weren't in a relationship. They weren't even dating; they were only pretend dating. So why should she care if he missed her?

As if on cue, her heart began to flutter as she got closer to the table. Even with the room pretty well packed, she picked Nick out with the surety of a wild bird seeking her mate within a flock of thousands. Her eyes stayed only on him.

He was standing with his back to her, but even from behind he stood out. His well-defined build and those tiny curls that teased the back of his neck made him instantly identifiable to her. With one hand in his pants pocket, the vented back of his tuxedo jacket pulled aside to reveal a wedge of black fabric stretched across his backside. He was speaking, gesturing with his free hand, revealing a band of white near his wrist beneath the black cuff of his jacket. Another band of white showed above his collar underlining his thick hair. Never again would she consider black a drab color. Not after seeing it stretched across the muscles of Nick.

She saw Nick's hand clap the man sitting next to him on the shoulder and then laugh. The sound of his laughter seemed to snake its way to her and wrap her in its rich tone. She smiled broader when she noticed that Trent was laughing too.

The last thought suddenly jabbed Somer like a bony finger in the ribs. *Trent was laughing. Why was*

*Trent laughing? Why was he even here?* This was bad. Very bad.

Nick turned in her direction and saw her, gesturing for her to join him. When he said something to the others at the table, they all turned toward her. It was only then that she noticed exactly who else was sitting at the table with them.

She knew her mouth had dropped open, but she had lost the strength to close it. They were all here; her mother, her brother, her sister, smiling at her as though she was the main course. And she might as well be. How in the world was she ever going to make it through the evening without being eaten alive?

The look on Nick's face in response to the one she probably had on her own was sheer confusion. His hand slowly came out of his pocket and then he smiled, greeting her like the date he was supposed to be.

She tried to move forward to join him but found her feet felt like they had been encased in cement. Fortunately Nick must have noticed too, because he shouldered his way to her, excusing himself as he rested his hand on a woman's elbow, gently easing her aside, all the while keeping his gaze on Somer.

He approached with both hands extended, palms up. "Somer, what's going on?" he whispered, still smiling. "You look like you're going to be sick."

Somer put her hands in his and leaned into him, kissing his cheek. "I just may be. What are they doing here?" she whispered into his ear.

"Aren't they supposed to be?"

"No."

"You didn't invite your family?"

Now Nick really looked confused. "It's not that I didn't invite them, I just didn't tell them," Somer replied. "I love my family, I really do. They're just . . ." She looked over his shoulder at them and waved at her mother. "They're complicated."

"Well if we stand here much longer, I suspect they're going to get a lot more complicated." He stepped to her side, his hand riding the shallows of her spine as he gently nudged her toward the table. "Shall we?"

Somer took a deep breath. "I feel like I'm walking into a pit full of hungry lions."

"You'll be fine," Nick reassured.

"How do you know that?"

"They've already had me as an appetizer."

## Chapter Fourteen

"Mom, what are you doing here?" Somer asked as Nick pulled out a chair next to Tess and waited for Somer to sit before reclaiming his seat. "And Trent and Ali?" She looked at each one as she said their names. "Charming." She had to force herself not to clench her teeth as she said the word.

"You don't seriously think we'd miss an opportunity like this, do you sister dear?" Trent cut in before Tess could answer Somer.

Somer shook her head and let a breath escape through her nose as she held her lips together to prevent one of the several smart remarks that were filling her head to escape. "I suppose I don't," she said once she regained control. She looked at Nick. He looked very confused. "I thought you were all busy," she said to her family.

"We thought we were," Trent continued, playing along to prolong Somer's agony, "but once Nick told us that the dinner was *this* week, we were *so* happy we could make it."

Somer turned to Nick. "So it was you who told them."

"Is that a problem?" Nick replied, brows still furrowed.

"We'll talk later," Somer said as sweetly as possible.

"Somerville, darling, you act as though you don't want us here," Tess said.

Apparently surprised by Tess's tone, Nick picked up his water glass to hide his lips and mouthed her name in a question. "Somerville?"

"Not at all, Mom," Somer replied, her eyes telling Nick to add that question to the one she had to discuss with him later. "I just know how hard it is for all of us to be on the same schedule."

"It's not every day my little girl gets an award."

"Mom, I'm thirty three."

"Not to Mom," Ali reminded.

The look on Ali's face told Somer that Ali was enjoying every minute of her discomfort, probably in retaliation for something she perceived Somer had done to her. "Then I guess that makes you the perpetual baby," Somer replied in a take-that tone.

Ali did not reply, but merely raised her glass in a salute of surrender. That worried Somer. Ali never gave up that easily.

"You do look beautiful dear," Tess said, smiling her approval at Somer. "Could it be because of Nick here?"

"I did have some highlights put in my hair last week," Somer replied, wanting to get the conversation off Nick as much as possible. "A few colors and a base. Like it?"

"You look more like Mom now," Ali tossed in.

"And that's a good thing," Nick said quickly. "Mrs. Archer hardly looks old enough to have three adult children." He slid his chair closer to Somer and put his arm around her. Somer tried to move away from him, but he held onto her shoulder. "Dear, you should have told me more about your family," he continued.

"I see you're schmoozing the potential in-laws," Trent said, baiting Somer as he snatched a piece of sushi from an hors d'oeuvre tray on the hand of a passing waiter.

"Now Trenton, from what Nick told us before Somer got here, that's a tad premature," Tess said, declining the offer of some tiny hot dogs rolled in pastry with a small swipe of her hand. "They've only been dating for a week or so now."

Somer finally managed to wiggle out of Nick's grasp. She leaned her elbow on the table and rested her chin in her hand. "What else have you told them, honey?"

"I really didn't spend much time alone with your family before you got here," Nick tried to reassure her. He gestured across the table. "By the way, have you met Leonard?"

Somer turned her attention to the man sitting across the table from her and nodded her greeting. So that was Leonard. He looked about the way she had expected him to look; cerebral, uncomfortable, and bookish. Despite her declaration that she was dating, Greg had apparently wanted to make sure she met Leonard anyway by seating him at her table. She'd speak to Greg about that later.

It was no wonder that Nick was acting all significant-otherly and possessive. She had asked him to run interference with Leonard, and that's exactly what he was doing. What a mess she had put herself in. Nick, her family, Leonard and a few different versions of the truth were all sitting at the table with her. If she got through the evening unscathed, she swore she'd never spin another yarn again.

Leonard made eye contact with her and she felt like a lunch special. She slid back and settled closer to Nick.

"So Leonard, your brother tells me that you're a rocket scientist," Somer said, trying again to shift the focus from her and Nick.

"Yeah, yeah, we found that out already," Ali said. "We want to know more about you and Nick."

"Exactly what has Nick told you?" Somer inquired.

"That he caught you going through his desk and it was love at first sight," Ali said.

Somer turned to Nick and smiled. "Is that what you told them?"

"No," Nick denied. "I mean I did tell them that I found you going through my desk."

"You don't believe in love at first sight, Nick?" Tess quickly asked.

"*Mom!*" Somer's voice carried to the next table where three people turned to see who was yelling.

"I think two people need to know each other for a while," Nick replied, taking Somer's hand. "And while I think your daughter is wonderful, she deserves the chance to know the person she falls in love with for more than a week." He felt Somer squeeze his hand in a gesture of thanks.

"But don't you agree that one can find themselves instantly attracted to another person on sight," Tess pressed.

"I do," Nick replied, turning his head so he could fully see Somer's face. He could tell she was working hard to keep her expression neutral.

"So then you do believe in love at first sight?" Ali asked, not allowing Nick an easy escape.

"To a point." Out of the corner of Nick's eye, he could see Somer's facial muscles tighten. It was time to get out of the conversation. "What do you think, Leonard?"

"Actually," Leonard said, turning his plate to position it to his liking, "many scientists think that love is linked to a chemical reaction in the ventral tegmental area and the caudate nucleus of the brain. As a matter of fact anthropologist Helen Fisher has devoted much of her career to studying the biochemical pathways of love in all its manifestations: lust, romance, attachment, the way they wax and wane." He cut the prime rib on his plate into bite-sized squares as he spoke.

"So then saying two people have a certain chemistry is not that far-fetched," Somer interjected, hoping that Leonard would go into lecture mode and take the family focus away from her and Nick.

Leonard nodded. "Although most people would probably be quite content with accepting this convention at face value, the truth is that the correlation between romance and thermodynamics runs quite deep."

"Do tell," Ali said, sounding positively bored.

Somer saw the opportunity to escape both the conversation and the table. "Just by chance, Ali has a friend who is looking for a research subject for her doctorate at Princeton. This topic sounds like something Lolly might find interesting. If you can synopsize this theory to Ali, then Ali can discuss it with Lolly as a possibility for her research thesis."

Leonard's face perked up for the first time since he sat down at the table. He inched his chair closer to Ali and pulled out a pen from the inside of his tuxedo jacket and retrieved the napkin from his lap. "Let us begin then with a theoretical chemical reaction where two elements, 'female' (F) and 'male' (M), combine to form a new compound called 'couple' (FM) or $F+M$——$>FM$," he said, writing the equation on the napkin.

Somer could see a bit of what he was scribbling down. It looked to her like algebra her high school teachers always told her she'd use someday. She never once thought that equations would apply to love.

"Usually M is the element with the higher atomic weight, although exceptions do exist," Leonard continued, completely in an element of his own now and apparently totally happy.

Ali, on the other hand, shot Somer a you're-going-to-pay-for-this look. Trent was trying to control a laugh that Somer suspected was going to break loose any minute and her mother did not look at all pleased with what Somer had just done.

And Nick looked perplexed. She'd have to spirit him away for a few minutes and explain that her family does this sort of thing to each other all the time.

Somer rose from her seat. "I need to check on

part of the program." She turned to Nick and gave him a slight head toss to tell him to join her.

Nick caught the body language. "And I need to make a quick call."

"Don't be long, dear," Tess said, "the ceremony will be starting soon."

"Wouldn't miss it," Somer said taking a step away from the table and thinking she was safe for a while.

But Ali had another idea. "Have you told Nick about the ring?" she asked, as Leonard turned over the paper he was writing on and jotted down his phone number.

"Ring?" Nick asked politely.

"Yes, Somer's grandmother's ring. She's supposed to use it to find the man of her dreams. Maybe that's why she met you so soon after she got it."

Nick swiveled to face Somer. "This is almost as interesting as Leonard's love theory."

Somer looked down at the steak left on her plate and wondered how it would look flattened on her sister's face. "We'll chat about that later," she promised Nick as she walked to Leonard and leaned down. "Leonard, did I mention that my sister, Ali, is unattached right now?" she whispered.

Leonard looked up from the paper. "No. No, you didn't." He looked at Ali and slid his chair closer to hers. She responded by sliding hers in the opposite direction. "Ms. Archer," he said to her. "Did you know that the brain chemistry of attraction could be akin to a mental illness?"

Ali watched her sister leave on Nick's arm. "No, but I'm sure I'm about to find out."

"Do you think you should have done that to your sister?" Nick asked when they reached the vestibule of the banquet room.

Somer waved off the question. "It's something we do to each other all the time."

"But what about Leonard? Aren't you giving him some false hope?"

"It'll be fine. Ali really does have a friend who is getting her doctorate at Princeton. Lolly, Lolotea, actually, a Zuni name meaning 'gift.' Lolly is a real intellectual. Leonard will love her. What happened in there is family tradition." Somer saw the puzzlement on Nick's face deepen. "Let me try to explain. Just like hanging mistletoe is to Christmas and fireworks are to the Fourth of July, sibling torture is much the same to the Archer family."

Nick seemed to sort out what Somer had just said before shaking his head. "Your family is quite the piece of work. And, by the way, what's with the naming of New Jersey cities? Somerville, Trenton. Another Archer family tradition?"

Somer rolled her eyes. "That's a story for later when we have more time."

Just then Trent appeared on his way to the parking lot.

"Leaving, I hope," Somer said when she saw him.

"Taking a break to get the camera. I *really* need to preserve this Kodak moment for the family archives," he replied, humor in his voice and in his eyes. "You have got to get back in there and watch Mooch and the mad scientist. It's priceless. He's up to about three napkins with all sorts of lines and circles on them. Looks like some kind of love flowchart." His laughter could be heard long after he closed the door behind him.

"Now that's a side of your brother I haven't seen yet," Nick commented.

"Yeah, sinister and evil. I've seen it a lot." She tipped her head. "It was kind of the same vibe I got from you when we first met."

"You thought I was sinister and evil?"

"Not in those words exactly. I thought you were hard-nosed and needed a lesson in humility," she said laughing. "Especially after the Chinese food thing."

He returned her laughter. "The tackle at the ball game was humbling enough." Out of the corner of his eye he saw Trent coming back. He reached out and put his arm around Somer, shifting her hip against his. "Show time," he whispered with a slight head toss in Trent's direction.

In return, Somer slipped her arm around Nick's waist and rested her hand on his chest. "I hope it isn't too painful pretending to be my date."

"I could get used to it," Nick assured with a wink. "You feel kind of nice. I could get used to that, too."

Trent stopped in front of them and clicked off a few pictures on his digital camera. "For the scrapbook." He paced around them like a paparazzi.

"Take one for me," Nick said suddenly.

As Trent centered the viewfinder, Nick circled Somer with both arms and pulled her securely against his body. As he dropped his head to kiss her, he pressed her hips against the rounded edge of the oak cabinet next to the staircase. "For my scrapbook," he whispered against Somer's mouth as he gently kissed her lips. His head moved and his hands pressed her back until he thought he heard a sigh of pleasure from behind her lips. Out of the corner of his eye he saw the flash of Trent's camera and pulled out of the kiss.

"Mom's going to love these," Trent joked as he used the screen on his camera to review his shots. He angled the camera to Nick and Somer. "Here's one for the inside of your locker at the station." It was the one of Nick kissing Somer.

Nick craned his head to see it, making sure he still held Somer prisoner between himself and the cabinet. "Make me a few five-by-sevens of that one," Nick said never taking his eyes from Somer's face. Then he looked back at Trent. "Then delete it permanently. I've been briefed on the family tricks," he cautioned.

"You better get back inside, Trent," Somer said running her fingertips under both of Nick's lapels. "We'll be back in a minute."

Nick went back to reviewing his shots on the camera as he walked away. "Oh, good one," he said angling the view screen toward Somer.

"I'll look at it later," she said, her gaze still on Nick.

"Not a problem," he replied, disappearing into the dining room.

"That was nice," Somer said after Trent left.

Nick leaned forward, his intentions written in the air around them. "I think it was a lot better than just nice."

"It might have been." Somer inhaled the scent of good cologne with a faint trace of ginger. To her it was the essence of masculinity. She wondered how many times she was going to look at the pictures her brother took and relive this kiss.

"The pictures should help convince your family that we're seeing each other."

*Was that all it was supposed to do?* Somer wondered, careful not to say the words out loud. Nick's motive behind kissing her was not the one she wanted to hear. She looked up at him and her breath caught as his gaze held hers with several lazy blinks of dark lashes.

And then her brain shut down with no chance of coming back on.

She circled his neck loosely with both hands. "Then this is really going to be convincing," she said right before she leaned back against the cabinet edge, pulling him with her. He felt solid against her hips again. She urged his head down, commanding him to kiss her again, this time with a full exchange of passion that grew into a greedy seeking of body pressure.

"A-hem!"

Somer and Nick broke contact like teenagers caught by parents. Trent stood in the archway to the banquet room, arms folded across his chest. "Break it up you two. The ceremony is about to start."

Somer felt the heat of color mounting in her chest and bathing her chin. "We were just on our way in."

Trent snorted. "I could see that. But before you do, your hair's a little messed up and most of your lipstick is on him." Trent pointed at Nick. "Not your color at all." Without another word he left them and disappeared into the banquet room.

Somer reached out and cupped Nick's chin, wiping the traces of her lipstick from his skin. "He's right. It's not your color."

Nick ran the back of his hand across his mouth, finishing the job. "I guess we're in for another round at the table."

"Probably." Somer kept her eyes on the broad

column of his neck while her pulse slowed to near normal. "We should probably go in before they send someone out to find us again."

"Unless you want to finish what we were doing before your brother interrupted us," Nick suggested, wagging his eyebrows up and down.

Though seriously tempted, Somer laughed off his suggestion. "In your dreams, Daultry."

As she walked by him to get to the banquet room, he took her hand and whirled her back into his arms. "Every night from today on," he said right before he kissed her again.

## Chapter Fifteen

Nick made sure his coffee lasted until the newspaper's publisher called Somer up to accept her award. He intended to keep his attention on her and listen carefully to her remarks so he could comment on them later, but as he looked at her, all of his senses converged on her face alone.

Somer was perfection to him. Physically and intellectually she seemed his equal, no, his complement. She was the kind of woman he'd been searching a long time for. At least from knowing her for only a little longer than a week he thought so. He didn't know how or why he felt that way, he just knew she had invaded his normally solitary space and he liked it.

She had a way about her; a strong, sure way in how she moved and walked and talked. She was a woman who needed and deserved a man who would challenge her, keep her interested, make her laugh, hold her when she was sad and plan the future with her when she was happy.

Just his luck to find her when he was on temporary assignment and due back in New York soon. How could he be sure what he was feeling wasn't just the safe thrill of the chase with a built-in excuse not to have to make a commitment after the catch? He had to be fair. To himself and to Somer.

Applause made him end deliberations on the subject as he watched Somer wind her way through the chairs and back to the table, engraved plaque in hand. He stood, intending to pull the chair out for her when she got to the table, but found himself taking her in his arms and planting a congratulatory kiss on her surprised mouth instead. He felt the surprise in her response soon turn to acceptance and smiled against her lips.

"Congratulations. You deserve it," he said over both the complimentary and teasing shouts of her family. Slowly he unwound his arms from around her. He pulled out her chair and waited until she sat before sitting next to her.

"A picture for posterity," Trent suggested, standing and pulling out the camera.

"I think you have taken enough for one night," Somer said tucking the plaque on the floor next to the chair.

Tess reached down and retrieved the award. "You should treat this with more respect, dear." She smiled at Nick. "Someday your children may want to know how their father met you and this plaque will be a very important piece in the story." She propped the award against the centerpiece. "There. Much better."

"Mom," the tone of the word warning as Somer spoke it. "It is a bit premature to talk about my children and their father."

Trent stood and tapped on his glass with a spoon. "Somer, Nick, family, I think a toast is in order." A white-shirted waiter moved around the table and set a fluted glass filled with champagne down in front of each of them.

Somer lifted her glass. "Where are Ali and Leonard?" She looked around the room but couldn't find them anywhere.

"Leo took Mooch outside. There's some sort of meteor shower that's supposed to happen tonight and he wanted to show her where to look," Trent replied.

"Leo?" Somer questioned.

"Mooch?" Nick asked about the same time.

"Shouldn't we wait for them?"

Trent answered Somer first. "Leonard is much too formal for this family. We decided to call him Leo instead." Somer simply shrugged at his explanation. Trent turned to Nick, "And Mooch, well, I'll let Sis tell you about that one later. As for waiting: naw. Mooch has no sense of direction so it's going to take an hour for Leo to get her to remember which way is north so she can see the meteors from the backyard later on tonight."

"Trenton! She's your sister," Tess protested. "Be nice."

"I was," Trent reassured. "If you weren't here I'd tell Nick what I really thought was happening outside."

Nick and Somer looked at each other and made a face in good humor, while Tess made one in disapproval.

"Anyway," Trent continued, "It goes without saying that we're all happy for you, Somer. You have a talent, a gift for writing. I remember how handy that came in during high school. You could write a mean absentee letter. They saved my butt more than once and I appreciate every one of them."

"And, I knew about every one of them," Tess said, merriment in her voice.

"You did?"

"Trenton, I always told you—no matter what you and your sisters ever did, I did it first and I did it better," Tess said matter-of-factly. "You cannot improve upon perfection."

Laughter rippled around the table.

"Somer," Trent began again, "We have a lot of fun in this family. We have teased you, tortured you, blamed things on you that you never did, but one thing we can all agree upon and that is we love you and we're proud of you." He lifted his glass momentarily higher. "To my sister, Somerville Alexa Archer, journalist extraordinaire. May the next prize you win have the word 'Pulitzer' in front of it." Glasses clinked as they met in the center of the table in agreement.

Nick touched the rim of his glass to Somer's. "I have no doubt that's going to be true," he said.

"Thanks," she replied. She sipped her champagne, but her eyes never left his. As the rim of his glass tipped up, her gaze remained steady on his arresting eyes until she thought she saw the sparkle of the champagne bubbles in their dark irises. A warm appreciative glow rose and she was glad she had asked him to pretend to be her date. She'd deal with explaining it to her family later. Right now, she was going to enjoy pretending it was real.

Nick eased his car behind Somer's in the driveway of her townhouse, conscious of the evening coming to an end and wishing there was more of it.

"Now that was an interesting date," Nick said turning off the engine.

"How gallant of you to put it that way," Somer replied.

"No, I'm serious. Your family, the awards dinner, it was interesting, all of it. I enjoy watching you interact with your brother and sister. And your mom, she sat there like the proud matriarch and enjoyed the whole thing."

Somer's eyes grew round and glittery. "It was kind of fun, wasn't it?"

She reached for the door handle on her side and Nick quickly popped the driver's side door open.

"Wait, I'll get that," he said.

She put her hand on his arm to stop him. "You don't have to do that. Gallant can stop at your assessment of our date and my family."

As she slid out of the car and closed the door, Nick's mind was screaming *Do something! Stop her.* He had opened his mouth to do just that when the passenger door reopened and Somer leaned back in.

"Do you want to come in?" she asked. "I was just going to watch some old movies on TV, but I think I should explain some things that happened at dinner instead. So you don't go back to the city and tell them about the weird family that inhabits the 'burbs."

"There are a few nagging questions," Nick agreed eagerly. He pulled out the keys and raised his eyes to the sky. "Thank you," he whispered to whatever force had just helped him. "I owe you one."

Inside, Somer ditched her purse and shoes and headed for the living room. Nick followed close behind.

"I'll get us some coffee in a minute." She sat down on the couch, crossed her left ankle over her right knee, took off her shoe and massaged her foot. "But you'll have to excuse me for a minute. You have no idea how much I hate wearing heels."

"You mean all the time from when I picked you up until we got back here your feet were aching?"

"I don't think my sneakers would have gone with the dress." She angled him a cute smirk. "But it would have been worth seeing the look on mom's face if I did wear them." She slipped the other shoe off. "Hope you don't mind. Archer women don't stand on formality most of the time." She wiggled her toes and stretched her legs out. "This feels so good."

Nick shoved the hassock from the brown chair next to the fireplace and sat down. "Here, give me a foot." Somer shrugged a what-the-heck motion, and extended her right leg to him. He captured her foot with his hand and rubbed it firmly.

The sensation shot a shiver up Somer's spine and she almost told him to stop. But the pressure on the aching muscles felt too good. Soon all she could concentrate on was the sensual feeling of his thumb massaging the arch of her foot.

"Mmmm, you're very good at that. Did they teach you that in cop school?"

"No, why?" Nick asked pressing her foot against his knee and covering it with his warm hand.

"Because at this point, if I were a suspect, I'd tell you anything if you promise not to stop."

"Okay then, tell me about your family. This sibling torture thing has me fascinated."

Somer dropped her head onto the back of the couch as he rotated her ankle. "Typical sister-brother-sister things. We just never outgrew them." She lifted her head. "What about you? No brothers or sisters to annoy?"

Nick shook his head. "Only child. Give me your other foot."

Somer laughed as she complied. "To keep me talking?"

"Yep. Now what about the city names? Are they nicknames or something?"

"Actually it's the other way around. Somerville is my given name; Trenton is Trent's."

Nick stopped massaging her foot. "Your parents named you after New Jersey cities?"

"With an explanation." Somer removed her foot from Nick's lap and sat up straight.

"I can hardly wait."

"My parents were hippies, flower children of the seventies. They were so in love and when they got married, they made a pact." She stopped, wondering how she was going to word what came next.

"And?" Nick coaxed after a few silent minutes.

"And they were so in love that they wanted to commemorate the places that contributed to their children's conception." She stopped again and waited for the words to sink in. It didn't take long.

The grin that broke across Nick's face made dimples in his cheeks that were deeper than Somer could have thought possible. "You mean you were named for the place that your mother and father . . ."

Somer held up a hand. "Stop right there." She dropped her hand and her head. "Not exactly. They named us after the place in which they decided the time was right to plan additions to the family. For me, it was my mom's twenty third birthday and they were celebrating."

"And your brother?"

"Anti-war protest."

To Nick's credit he didn't quite laugh out loud. "Okay, I get it. But your sister, Ali. I noticed that Trent calls her Mooch. What's that all about?"

Somer gave a most unladylike snort. "Hers is the best of all. Mom and Dad were at a reunion of a few of their friends. The get-together was in a beautiful state park in Northern New Jersey's Skylands. Most of their friends still had babies. I was nine and Trent was seven. Mom got sentimental."

"I don't know New Jersey that well," Nick said, "but I can tell by the look on your face this is going to be good."

Somer nodded, barely containing her own laughter. "It was Allamuchy State Park. So my baby sister is Allamuchy Tessa Archer. Mom and I call her Ali, Trent calls her Mooch."

"No wonder she seems so angry." His burst of laughter matched Somer's. "Okay so that answers most of my questions," he continued when their laughter finally died, "but what's this ring thing Ali was talking about?"

Somer let herself fall back on the sofa. "I was afraid you were going to ask that." She lifted one delicate eyebrow. "Are you sure you want to hear it?"

"How bad could it be?"

Somer slapped her thighs with her palms. "Okay. A few weeks ago my mother calls a family meeting." She tossed her head. "In our family, meetings are like calls to doom; something always seems to happen to one of us because of them."

"Sounds like a Steven King novel."

"Could very well be. Anyway, we get there and Mom is like all June Cleaver; hair in a bun, house dress, apron, very un-Tess-like. We quickly find out that she has decided she wants grandchildren and sets us out on a quest to have some."

"Interesting," was all Nick could say.

"It gets better," Somer warned. "Mom pulls out three of my grandmother's favorite rings and gives one to each of us with the instructions that they would help us find our other half so we could get moving on her grandchildren.'

"Very interesting," Nick repeated.

"Very bizarre, you mean."

Nick looked around the room as if he was waiting for someone or something to jump out at him. "So where is this ring now?"

Somer reached out and patted his hand. "Don't worry. We don't give much credence to the whole ring prophecy thing. You're perfectly safe."

"Can I see it?"

"No. It's in the freezer."

Nick looked confused. "In the freezer," he repeated.

"Just in case. If it has some magical karma attached to it, I'd like to see it get through ice."

"Ah-ha."

Somer threw up her hands. "So there you have it. The Archer family. Crazy as loons. And now that you know about the ring curse, aren't you glad that we actually aren't dating?"

Nick didn't hesitate. "No."

Somer's quick intake of breath preceded a long stretch of silence while Nick looked at her upturned face, bathed in the golden light from the lamp next to the couch. Her chest rose and fell as her heartbeat raced with the intensity of his gaze.

He raised his hand and brushed her hair back from her cheek with a tenderness that made her nearly forget to take another breath. "I'd like this to have been a real date," he said.

"Even with what I just told you?"

"Especially with what you just told me. Your family is great, Somer. They're fun, fascinating. I guess at times they can really exasperate you, but I can tell from tonight that you all love each other very much, and that's something special." His thick dark lashes lowered as his gaze fell to her mouth.

"Thanks," she whispered, her own gaze falling to his lips.

His hand rose again, this time to her neck where his fingers curled into her hair, cupping the back of her head. His gaze rose to her eyes and he stared, a steady stare that felt as if he could see right into her heart. There was so much tenderness there that she felt the warmth down to her soul.

Without thinking anymore she grabbed two handfuls of his shirt and pulled herself forward, pressing her mouth to his until she felt him groan and match her move for move. Deep into the kiss, their heads moved from side to side while his fingers moved against the back of her neck. His other hand snaked around her waist to hold her so tight that she could barely breathe.

After what didn't seem long enough to her, Nick leaned his head back and her eyes flicked back to his face. She let her gaze fall from the wave of hair that fell across his forehead, past the dark eyebrows to the deep green of his eyes to the smooth flush on his skin. The sensual sweep of his mouth was curled into a smile.

"Now I've gone and done it, haven't I?" she asked.

Nick leaned forward and kissed her gently. "Yes you have," he said against her lips.

"We're going to miss the meteor shower aren't we?"

"Uh-huh," Nick said, "and probably the movie, too."

Nick looked down at Somer. She was nestled in the crook of his arm, her feet tucked underneath her on the couch. Without much movement so he wouldn't disturb her, he looked at his watch. It was three A.M. They had fallen asleep watching TV and missed the meteor shower.

He moved slightly so he could see her better. Her hand rested on his chest, her blond hair cascading across the arm he had around her shoulder. She never looked more beautiful to him as she did now; peaceful, almost vulnerable like someone he would protect at all costs.

He moved a tendril of hair away from her face and marveled at the way her dark lashes shadowed her cheeks. He thought he could look at her like this forever.

But it was getting late. He bent his head and pressed his lips to her forehead. "Somer, honey, I have to go."

She stirred and then blinked her eyes open. "How long have I been asleep?" she asked, pushing away from him. "Last thing I remember is *Carousel* coming on right after *On the Waterfront*."

"You drifted off halfway through the chick-flick,"

he said feeling cooler air hit his side, erasing the warmth Somer had made there. He didn't like the feeling.

"It was only fair that the guest pick the movie we watch first," she said rubbing her eyes with the back of her had. "So what time is it?"

"It's three," he said.

She yawned and stretched. "Sorry to keep you here so long. You should have woken me." She rose and looked down at her horribly wrinkled dress. "The dry cleaner is going to have a lot of work ahead of him with this one."

"I should go." Nick stood and gathered her back into his arms. When he did, he felt warm again. Warm and at home.

They walked arm in arm to the door. Nick gathered his coat and put it on. Somer looped the black bow tie around his neck but didn't bother to tie it. Slowly she let her fingers fall down his chest before they stopped at his sides.

"This was nice," she said, smiling up at him. "Thank you."

Nick stared at her, clearly mystified. "For what?"

"For tonight. For agreeing to be my date, for dealing with my family and for," she lowered her lashes and then snapped them back up, "for now."

Nick pulled her to him. She rested her head on his chest as he stroked her hair. "It was my pleasure, Somer."

She could feel his tension. With her head resting on his solid chest, she could hear the rhythm of his racing heart. When his fingers tangled in her hair and he tilted her face up for the touch of his lips, the warmth he had brought into her life exploded into a raging fire. Wondering became desire. Doubts fled, replaced by certainty.

And still he let her go.

His eyes never left hers but they were filled with raw excitement. "I don't want to leave," he said, holding her in a loose embrace, his hands resting lightly on her hips.

Somer's breath caught in her throat and she saw the control in his expression. She knew he would never ask for more until he was sure there was more to their relationship than just attraction.

"But I will," he said, his hands falling to his sides. "We both have a lot of work to do in the morning, which, if my math skills haven't been scrambled, is only about four hours away."

"Will I see you then?"

"I'll stop by the newspaper after breakfast. We should sit down and see what we have on the black car and the B and Es. Maybe we can put our heads together and come up with some answers."

"Sounds promising," Somer said with deliberate suggestiveness.

Nick shook his head. "Good night, Somer." Then he kissed her. Chastely and on the cheek.

She began to close the door after him when she stopped. Was it her imagination or was the song he was whistling as he walked away the same one that Billy Bigelow and Julie Jordan sang to each other in the famous scene of the very movie during which she had fallen asleep—"If I Loved You." *Couldn't be,* she decided. *Carousel* was definitely not Nick's type of movie and if she was a betting woman, she'd wager he probably preferred Tim McGraw's country twang to show tunes.

Only after she closed the door and had time to think about it did she decide that Nick had actually been very wise leaving as he did. Any more kissing would only complicate things more than they already had.

Suddenly some of the lyrics of the song drifted in and around her mind.

"But afraid and shy I'd let my golden chances pass me by. Soon you'd leave me; off you would go in the mist of day. Never, never to know. That I . . ."

She gave her head a shake. This was silly. No one loved anyone in just short of two weeks. The song probably stuck in her head subconsciously while she slept. That's all it was. They had work to do and they had lives to lead. His was in New York. Hers was here.

Or was it?

Spending tonight with Nick had told her a lot about the state of her emotions where he was concerned. A part of her wanted to seriously explore the possibilities posed while another part feared they might just be moving onto dangerous turf. That was the part that was grateful that Nick had left.

But, she feared, the other part probably would be singing that silly song all night and not let her get to sleep because the lyrics has worked their way back, loud and strong.

"Words wouldn't come in an easy way. 'Round in circles I'd go!"

She gave in and sang the song once, twice, twenty times before putting the pillow over her head. When she finally did drift off, she was plunged into some very wonderful dreams.

When she awoke, she felt strangely energized considering she only had about three hours' sleep. While she first gave the credit to going to the gym and eating healthily, she finally had to admit that maybe it did have a little something to do with Nick.

## Chapter Sixteen

Somer sat at her desk in the newspaper office, sure something had changed between her and Nick. She felt it. She wondered if Nick felt it, too. At one point during the evening it had crossed her mind that she should have stopped what was happening. She should have taken a moment to slow down and talk to Nick about what she was feeling.

But it felt so right to be with him that it was too darn hard to resist. It was when she woke up on the couch in his arms that the magnitude of what had been happening to her really hit.

She never felt more connected to someone in her life. Not physically and not emotionally. She couldn't ever remember having such a deep sense of contentment being around someone. It was like Nick was made for her.

It was like love at first sight.

But it couldn't be that simple, could it? Could one person actually have a soul mate they could instantly recognize? Meeting Nick had been that and so much more.

But before she could take the time to think it all through, Greg came into the office.

"Here you go, hot off the presses." He said sliding the morning edition onto her desk. "You don't take too bad a black and white picture."

Somer scooped the paper up. Her picture was top right on the first page. "Great. Just what I didn't want; my face in every newspaper vending machine in the county."

"It's good publicity for the paper," Greg returned.

"I'd rather remain in the background."

"Not today. It's your fifteen minutes. Enjoy them."

Another voice joined the conversation. "Am I interrupting something?" Nick stood in the doorway, two cups of coffee in a cardboard carrier in one hand, a bag of donuts dangling from his other. He walked to Somer and placed a light kiss on her cheek. "Because I can come back later."

Greg held up his hands in a defensive posture. "Far be it from me to get in the way. I was just showing Somer her picture in this morning's edition."

Nick slid breakfast onto Somer's desk. "Let me see." He took the paper from Somer's hand and angled it to get a better look. "You look great, honey."

"Thanks," she replied as Greg left them alone. She studied Nick's face for a long moment, wondering if she would ever get tired of seeing those great dimples. "You don't have to play along being the boyfriend any longer. He's gone."

"I don't think I am playing."

With a flicker of her lashes, Somer looked away from him. Should she ask him what he meant by that? She could start talking about how she felt a connection with him after last night, but maybe she was moving a bit too fast.

Nick removed the lid from his coffee and took a healthy swig. "I hope you have some milk around here because I forget to ask for some for you."

"Black's fine. Thanks."

"I thought you might like a little snack while we brainstormed about the B and Es."

Somer paused for a breath. He sounded much too casual for her. She ditched the idea of talking to him about anything but the case. She reached over and pulled a chair from the next desk closer to hers. "What have you got?"

Nick turned the chair around so the back of the chair faced her and sat, legs straddling the seat, arms resting casually on top of the chair back. While he listed what he had, Somer could only stare at him. His latent maleness was playing havoc with her senses.

"We have the black car and the connection between the driver and the mayor's son. We have the mayor at a place he normally doesn't go, doing something he normally doesn't do, with him admitting the car was there. We have a locked shed in the backyard of the mayor's house with newly painted windows so no one could look inside."

Somer blinked at him. "Without hard proof, it's all conjecture at this point."

"And we have this." Nick reached into the pocket of the jacket he was wearing and pulled out an iPhone wrapped in a plastic evidence bag. "I checked with the phone company and this phone was listed as stolen after the second break-in."

"Where did you get it?"

"On the ground outside that shed."

"Why didn't you tell me about it?"

"Because you came running up the driveway, the mayor's wife came home suddenly and later, I got a bit distracted."

Somer took the phone from his hand. "What did you find out about it?"

"It belongs to the owner of the second house that was broken into. One of the detectives from the county ran it through the new forensics lab and found some sediment and a partial print. I'm on my way to see if it's enough for a warrant to search the shed."

Somer jumped up. "What are we waiting for then? Let's go."

Nick's hand settled on her arm and pulled her back to sitting. "*We* aren't going anywhere. I'm going to court; you're staying here." He kept his hand on her arm so she couldn't get away. "It could take a few hours to get the warrant." Somer nodded as Nick got up and returned the chair to the other desk. "I'll call you when and if I get it."

"I want an exclusive," she said.

A teasing glint came into Nick's eyes. "I'll try to get you one for the story. You already have one for me."

For a brief moment, Nick saw thoughts about his comment cross her eyes. Then a sparkle began in their blue depths and a smile teased the corners of her lips.

"We'll have to talk more about the last one," she said.

"That we will," Nick returned. He saw her face brighten and her lips part in a wider smile that showed her teeth. A sudden wild desire to keep that look on her face gripped him. Even if it meant changing everything he thought he knew.

Somer was worth it.


A mere five minutes after Nick left, Somer missed him. She wondered what it was about him that made her feel so connected to him. At her age, it certainly wasn't just some sort of crush. She'd never met anyone before who had caught her attention so fully. For her it was a massive thing, and she liked it.

He'd hinted that he felt the same. At least that's what she thought he had done. She had three weeks to find out for sure. Three weeks. Not a very long time. Even shorter if they had to use most of it to dig up more leads to solve the case.

But if the case was solved . . .

Somer grabbed her camera. Nick could wait for a judge to issue the search warrant if he wanted. As a cop, he'd have to go down every legal avenue or else take a chance of any evidence found in the shed being declared inadmissible.

But as a reporter, she really didn't adhere to quite the same set of rules. As an investigator, she could go to the mayor's house just to ask him a few questions. If she was looking for him around the back of his house and accidentally broke a window in the shed, she'd have to look inside to see if anyone might have gotten cut by the broken glass. If no one was in the shed, she'd have to take a picture so she could tell if any of the contents had been damaged. And if the pictures just happened to show what could be some of the stolen merchandise, well that would definitely be grounds for a search. Then Nick could get the warrant and crack the case.

True, he told her to stay put, but she knew his gratitude for her help would certainly overshadow the fact she didn't listen to him.

At least that's what she told herself as she turned on the ignition and pulled the car out of the parking lot, heading for the mayor's house. Though she felt torn about possibly having to break into the shed, she knew if she found something, it would help Nick with the case.

As she drove there, she thought she'd run variations of Nick's theory through her mind. Though she tried to concentrate on the possibilities of the investigation, it was the possibilities with Nick that kept coming to mind.

"Go away for a few minutes, Daultry," she whispered. But as she expected, he paid no attention to her. Visions of his face plagued her with the look she thought he'd have when he discovered what she's been up to. "Okay, okay," she conceded. "I'll tell you what I find just as soon as I find it. Then you can handle it from there."

She had just made the left onto the street when she saw the notorious black car pull out of the mayor's driveway. Now she had a decision to make; check out the shed as planned or follow the car.

The shed wasn't going anywhere. Throwing caution to the wind, she passed the driveway and went straight. For about five miles she maintained a showdown distance between them before a series of turns left her at an intersection with nothing ahead of her but the dusk of the coming night.

She thumped her palms on the steering wheel. "I couldn't have lost him." But she had. Left, right, straight. Which way now? She'd just made her decision when she was hit from behind, her car first jerking forward on impact and then sliding to the right, narrowly missing the stop sign.

As the force of the contact threw her first frontward into the steering wheel and then bounced her back into the driver's seat, she managed a look in the rearview mirror.

The driver of the black car had somehow gotten behind her, and, if her instincts were still working, he was not at all happy about her following him. She straightened the car and jammed her foot onto the accelerator intent on making a quick getaway.

But the driver of the car behind her did the same, keeping pace with her speed and movements as they raced down the center of the darkening street. The zoning in this area was ten acres per house, so there weren't many homes close to the street, not much of a chance for people to see her racing and call the police.

She leaned on her horn, hoping to attract attention. She looked in the rearview mirror and saw that the black car was gaining on her. She pressed even harder on the accelerator, feeling as though her foot would go through the floorboard any second. She grabbed the wheel with both hands and glanced again into the rearview mirror as the headlights of the car behind her illuminated the inside of her car.

He was going to hit her again and there was no way for her to avoid it.

## Chapter Seventeen

When the car hit hers, Somer slammed on the brakes and threw her hands up in front of her face to shield her eyes against the force of the airbag deploying. Somehow the windshield also shattered, and she could feel shards of glass prickling her skin before the bag filled completely. Warm dampness, she knew without looking, was blood running down her hands. Her stomach lurched with the feeling.

Her foot slipped from the brake to the accelerator and the car hurled forward. Without her hands on the steering wheel to guide it, the car skidded toward the shoulder of the road. Flashes of trees blurred as she looked out the side window and the scent of pine filled the air when branches broke with the force of the impact.

Fighting with the airbag, she grabbed the steering wheel and hit the brakes as hard as she could. She jerked the wheel to the left to try to prevent the car from sliding down the embankment just beyond the tree line and into a canal that had been used in colonial days to get goods to the river a few miles away. Thankfully, the brakes caught and the car jolted to a stop.

Switching off the ignition with a trembling hand, she slid down in the seat and waited. A cold trickle of perspiration ran down her back. Her heart thudded. She wondered if the driver of the car would possibly come down to see if she were hurt or to make sure she was. But after a few minutes, she heard the rev of an engine and a car speed off.

She wasn't sure how long she sat there, frozen by shock, too numb to try and get out of the car. Her pulse finally began to slow and then a male voice made her jump and sent her heart rate soaring again. She realized it was just the operator from the Mobile Assist that came with her car asking her if she was all right. She gave him the details and he instructed her to not move while he dispatched help.

Before a new wave of angst could wash over her, Somer tried to recall every single detail of the incident so she could help the police with their investigation. But she was surprised about how little she remembered. The fear must have dimmed her powers of observation because the only thing she was certain about was that the car that hit her was black. She remembered following it, but not where she lost it. No image of the driver came to her mind, no suggestion of how she had let it get behind her. She was a reporter. A good reporter. Heck, she'd just won an award for a story wrought with details. And now she had none.

Infuriated by her own inadequacy, she drew in a deep breath and reached for her purse. Without pausing to wipe away the streaks of blood on her hands, she called Nick. She wasted no time with pleasantries when he answered.

"This is Somer. Can you check out the nine-one-one call that just came in about an accident and go there?" She stopped and listened to his question. "Because I'm the one who was in it, and I'll need a ride home."

He must have heard the quiver in her voice because he told her that he was on his way and hung up before she could respond.

Somer sat on the steps in the back of the ambulance when Nick burst around the police car blocking the road. The police car's light rack and the ambulance's emergency lights flashed in alternating time, making her look even more pale than she was. An EMT had just cleaned blood from her hands, but some still stained her blouse.

He nearly ran over some uniformed officers on his way to her. He took her in his arms for a minute to assure himself she was not badly injured.

With a sound that seemed like relief mixed with anger he took a step backward and assessed every part of her with the trained eye of someone who had seen too much in his career. "Are you all right?" His hands ran down her arms, his fingertips examining as they did. "Where are you hurt?"

"Just a few cuts on my hands. Nothing serious."

"An accident is always serious." He pulled her back into his arms and rested his chin on her forehead. "Don't ever scare me like this again."

Somer rested her head on his shoulder and enjoyed the safe circle of his arms. "I was trying to help."

Nick closed his eyes and held her for a moment before speaking. "I know."

"Did you happen to see my car on the way over here?" she asked so he would not start to lecture her on listening to him when he tells her to stay put.

Nick's gaze narrowed as he took in her ashen complexion, the trail of blood on her shirt and arms and the faint hysteria in her voice. His voice dropped to a gentle tone she had never heard before. "Tell me what happened."

"Just go look at the car."

"Why?"

"Please. It's important."

He hesitated, his eyes filling with concern. "Will you be okay?"

Somer looked at the young EMT taking the blood pressure cuff from her arm. "I'm sure Dr. Kildare here will keep an eye on me."

"She has trouble listening," Nick said to the EMT as he backed away. "I'd tie her down if I were you."

He was gone for all of three minutes. Somer timed him using the second hand on her watch. His eyes blazed and tension lines that weren't there before had appeared around his lips as though he were waging a battle to stay calm. The restrained anger came out in his tone when he rephrased the question he asked earlier.

"Would you care to tell me what happened here?"

Somer's fear turned to anger with the tone of his voice. "You're the detective. You tell me."

"I thought you said that rural America was safe," he shot back as he approached. "Is she okay?" he asked the EMT when he was closer to them.

"A few cuts from the glass," he answered, "and she may be stiff and a little sore in the morning from being bounced around in the car, but basically, she's not hurt."

"Shouldn't she get checked out at the hospital?"

"Won't go."

Somer met Nick's disbelieving gaze and tried a wavering smile. "I'm fine. Really. I'm just short on the details. I think I got run off the road, but I could be mistaken. Maybe a car cut me off. I hear taxis in New York do it all the time."

Nick ignored the sarcastic comment. "Is that what your reporter side thinks happened?"

Suddenly drained and tired of trying to be brave, Somer's shoulders slumped. "No, I think someone ran me off the road on purpose. That's why I wanted you to look at the car before it got towed."

"Someone did." His voice was very soft. He held out a piece of custom grillwork. "I found this on the road. It's obviously not from your car." Anger bubbled in his voice. "A few more feet and you would have been careening down the side of this precipice and into the canal. You could have been killed."

Nick began to pace. When he looked at her, she could see the warmth and concern in his eyes. Despite her best efforts to be brave, tears spilled down her cheeks. Nick was back at her side in an instant, his arms tight around her. She buried her face in the front of his shirt and sobbed.

"Don't cry, Somer," he said. "We'll get whoever did this." He murmured soothing words as he kissed her forehead and stroked her hair.

"I don't want to cry," she said between heaves of her chest. "I'm just so mad.

"And scared."

"I am not scared."

"Just relax and tell me exactly what happened."

Though it wasn't exactly a professional police interrogation, to her amazement, Nick evoked details from her that she never thought she would remember. He had all the right street-wise instincts and asked all the right questions. But there was a certain gentleness and compassion that softened the hard edges she thought came with being a New York City cop.

"Do you believe me now when I tell you that this isn't some kid's game?" Nick asked when he was finished.

"I'll concede that point," Somer said more softly than she would have liked.

"And you're going to cooperate and do what I ask you?"

"For a while."

"I'm going to get a patrol officer to take you home," he said standing.

"I don't need a . . ."

Nick raised his hand, stopping her.

She nodded once, acquiescing to the gesture.

"Just one more thing," he said.

"What's that?"

"What have you been doing since I told you to stay put earlier today?

Somer sighed. "Let's see. I picked up lunch. Went to the dry cleaners. Met my deadline for tomorrow's edition." She pressed her lips together. "That's about it."

Nick shook his head. "I don't believe you. What else?"

"I went to the mayor's house to check out the shed," she mumbled into her hand.

"I didn't quite catch that."

"I went to check out the shed."

Nick folded his arms across his chest. "And?"

"But when I got there, the black car was pulling away from the house so I followed it."

"What were you thinking, Somer?"

"I was thinking that the evidence was probably in the shed and, if I got it, I could help you crack the case. Isn't that how it works in New York? The police work with reporters and informers to get the information they need to make an arrest." Her next words were out before she could stop them. "Then we'd have more time together before you left."

So were his. "I wouldn't allow anyone I cared about to put themselves in danger for me again."

"Again?" Somer asked softly.

Nick seemed to stiffen. "This is not the time to talk about it." He gestured to a patrol officer standing nearby. "Take Ms. Archer home," he said. "And make sure she doesn't leave her house until I get there."

The officer nodded and stepped back so Somer could cross in front of him to get to his patrol car.

"I mean it Somer," Nick said as she passed him. "Stay home. I'll get there as soon as I can."

She turned to him. "I will."

For the first time since he got there, Somer thought she saw his shoulders relax. "It's about time," he said as he walked toward her car.

## Chapter Eighteen

It was a very long wait as far as Somer was concerned. She was frustrated by her failed attempt to help Nick with the investigation. Now the only story she could write with any certainty was the one on her own ineptness.

She heard his car and opened the door before he knocked. "I'm sorry," she said, stepping back as he came inside. "I know I screwed up, so don't lecture me."

"You didn't," he said, sitting on her sofa and patting the cushion next to him meaning for her to sit down.

"I didn't?" She folded one leg under and sat next to him.

"When I was at the accident scene I got a call telling me that the search warrant had gone through. I met a detective from the county prosecutor's office at the mayor's house and we cut the lock on the shed. It was packed full of stuff, we think from the robberies. Some detectives are there now logging it all in as evidence."

Somer let her head fall onto the back of the couch. "I should have waited."

"Yep, you should have."

She sat back up. "You could sugar-coat it to make me feel better."

"We'll get to that in a minute. Anyway, the mayor and his son came out of the house with his lawyer."

"I told you, there are no secrets in rural America."

"There are no secrets anywhere," Nick acknowledged. He took her hand and rubbed his thumb across her knuckles.

"If you're trying to distract me, you're doing a good job," Somer teased. "And you're raising an entirely different line of thought, though one with equally unresolved questions."

"We'll get to that later, too," Nick acknowledged. "But for now, back to the case. The mayor's lawyer said the son, Matt, was willing to make a deal. I said it would be based on any information that was supplied and he turned on the Carson kid right there in the driveway."

"The black car."

"And apparently the mastermind. It started as a kid's joke that got out of hand."

"How so?"

"The first B and E was at the star quarterback's house. It seems Matt Brown had been burnt by the quarterback and wanted to get even. He just wanted to teach the kid a lesson. They had every intention of dumping any stuff they took where it could be found, but when they broke into the kid's house and found a lot of trendy electronics, James decided to keep most of it. Some stuff he kept, some stuff he sold."

"That explains the tricked out Camaro."

"James got greedy and wanted more. He threatened to go to the police if Matt didn't help him pull off a few more jobs. Matt knew that he would ruin his father's political career if what happened hit the papers."

"What happened would have been in every political flyer on every doorstep in town. The mayor would never be elected to office ever again. I told you small town politics was brutal."

"That you did," Nick agreed.

"So the boys kept the loot in the shed behind the mayor's house figuring no one would ever look there."

"But someone did stick her pretty nose where it didn't belong. Carson recognized you from the story about your journalism award. When he saw you at the mayor's house, he got spooked and didn't know what to do."

"So he ran me off the road."

"To try to scare you into backing off."

"Did you arrest him, too?"

Nick nodded. "When I went to his house after making sure Matt and his parents got to the station, he gave himself up."

"He didn't even try to run?"

"Couldn't. The Camaro was all banged up in the front with a whole lot of paint transfer from hitting the back of your car. Forensics will match up the paint to prove it was him."

"What about the bank robbery?"

"Your theory was right. The mayor went there to meet James to try to talk him into turning himself in with a promise that the mayor would foot the legal fees. Unfortunately the bank was robbed while they were in the parking lot, drawing attention to the mayor being there."

"And James got spooked and nixed the deal."

"Apparently so."

"And when I pressed the mayor about it at the restaurant, he did panic and talk about the black car."

Nick nodded. "You were right about that, too."

"But the bank robbery is still an open case."

"But not ours any longer. Some of the stolen money was passed in a store in Pennsylvania. Since the money crossed state lines, it's a federal case now. They'll handle it from here on."

"So it's over?"

"Seems to be."

Somer slouched back. "Wow. This is like something you'd see on 'CSI.' "

"Not quite as dramatic, but close."

"You're a heck of a detective, Daultry."

"I couldn't have done it without your help."

Somer was surprised by the hint of distress in his voice. "You sound as though you're sorry about that."

"Not sorry exactly. Upset that I had to learn about myself by involving you."

"What do you mean?" She didn't like the direction in which this conversation was heading.

"Remember what I said that I didn't want someone I cared about being put in danger again?"

"Yes." Her voice sounded small and worried.

"I didn't tell you everything about how I got hurt in New York."

Somer closed her eyes for a moment and then snapped them open. "So tell me now."

"I told you that I got knifed pulling a punk off my partner. What I didn't tell you was that I made a stupid rookie mistake that night. There had been a rash of good samaritan crimes in the area. I knew the MO; I should have known what we came across could have been a set-up, but I didn't wait for backup. Before I knew it, there was a scuffle, and I saw some guys jump her. I dragged them off her just as I heard the sirens of the back-up units, but somehow I ended up with a knife in my shoulder."

"You saved her."

"I wouldn't have had to if I didn't let her put herself in danger just to make a collar."

"I'm sure she didn't see it that way."

"But I did." His rich green eyes were partially hidden behind half closed lids, their long lashes creating needle-like shadows on his cheeks as he continued to brush a thumb lightly over the back of her hand. "And it almost happened again today. I almost lost someone I care very much about."

"But you didn't."

She started to move toward him, but he stopped her. "Let me just sit here and look at you for a while."

She nodded and sat perfectly still, allowing his gaze to roam over her face. She watched his eyes settle on her mouth, then rise to her eyes before moving across her face to settle back on her mouth again.

And while he gazed, she did some looking of her own. She looked at his face, his hair, the line of his jaw and knew she would never tire of them. She recalled the sound of his laughter, the teasing hint in his voice. The time they had spent together over the last few weeks had been some of the happiest in her life. She smiled as she realized she loved him.

"Until I met you," he continued, "I never felt such a rapport with anyone. It feels right just to share the sun with you during the day and the cool air in the evening. I feel like I can tell you anything."

She reached out and cupped his cheek. "You can, Nick. I feel the same way, too."

"Then I have to tell you. I'm going back to New York."

"I know," Somer replied, "the program is over in three weeks."

"No. Tomorrow."

"Tomorrow?" The word came out in a rush of breath.

Nick nodded. "Part of the reason I came here was that after the shooting I felt powerless, like no matter what I did, nothing would ever change. Then I met you and found out I was wrong. Everything we do contributes to change; good and bad. Meeting you has changed me forever, Somer. I'm a better person, stronger, more sure of myself, and it's all because of you. I thank you for that."

"You're welcome, I think." She dropped her head and blinked to stop the tears that were building in her eyes. "Wow, you're breaking up with me and we never even dated. That has to be a first."

Nick laughed. To Somer it sounded forced. "There's something else I need to thank you for," he said

"What's that?"

"For making me a believer in love at first sight."

As they looked at each other, Somer's tears broke

loose. Nick put his arms around her and held her loosely, rocking back and forth as if trying to soothe her. His unsmiling lips moved as he spoke. "You feel it too, don't you?"

"Yes." There was no need to clarify her answer.

"We could be great together, you and I."

"I think so, too, Nick."

"But I have to go back."

"Yes, I know."

"You can come with me," he said, half a statement, half a question.

Somer shook her head. "No, I can't. Everything I am is here. New York is like a big all-you-can-eat buffet filled with everything you want to sample. But it's not something for everyday. Not for me anyway."

"I could stay here."

"No, you can't. I know how the city can get under your skin. I doubt if there's any other city in the world that offers so much. You'd never be happy here. Except for the excitement of this last case, the most crime we ever have here is cow tipping. And now that I've seen firsthand how you handle a victim and an investigation, I know someone like you would be wasted here, and it would be all my fault. I can't do that to you. I won't."

"So we'll date via Amtrak."

Somer shook her head. "No, we won't. Oh, it would be good for a while, but after a few weeks of schedules, delays and time tables, the commute would become something we dreaded."

"I'll drive here then."

Somer narrowed her eyes. "Have you taken a good look at your car? It'll last two weeks on the turnpike, if the bumper-to-bumper traffic on Route 287 doesn't get it first. Pretty soon you'll stop coming here on Fridays and then weekends will be postponed." She shook her head. "No, we can't waste time like that. Not with the jobs we have."

"It wouldn't be a waste of time, Somer," Nick protested. "New York's not that far."

"For accountants and financial consultants who work nine to five. Not for cops and journalists who work twenty-four-seven just to see what they start through to the end no matter what and no matter how long it takes."

"I can make time."

Somer chuckled. "For a while you will. I would, too. We might even put up with the commute. For a while. The trains are packed, drivers on the turnpike are crazed and we won't even talk about the buses." She crossed her arms over her chest and took two steps away from him. "And let's not even get into the time you need to solve some of those city cases, or the time I need to research my stories. We'll end up seeing each other less and less and making excuses why it has to be that way. Each of us will pretend it's all right while we end up feeling more guilt than affection. We'll make excuses or see each other when we really don't want to because we feel a responsibility to." She closed her eyes and shook her head. "No. We can't let any of that happen." She opened her eyes and looked at him. "So we aren't going to start something we will have to end." She wiped a tear that trailed down her cheek with her fingertips. "Let's just remember this time as something special."

Nick rose and pulled her to him. When he spoke, his voice was thick with apology and muffled against her neck. "I am so sorry, Somer. I don't want to hurt you."

"You aren't," she lied. "Reporters and cops—oil and water. Each one following leads to the exclusion of everything else no matter where it takes then. We proved that. I got the story and you found yourself." She laughed. It was more a disjointed nervous snicker than anything else. "No, it wasn't love at first sight. It was just something different for both of us."

Nick's eyes looked tormented when he nodded.

"Don't blame yourself. It was the excitement of it all; the crime, the chase, the fantasy. It wasn't just you who got caught up in it all. It was both of us." He stood silent and unmoving. "It was fun, though."

Again he just nodded and then looked at her briefly before standing and walking to the door with her. When she turned the knob, the sound was like a sonic boom in the silence.

"Good-bye Nick," Somer said, placing her lips lightly on his.

He stepped through the door, and as she closed it behind him, he lurched, as if waking from a dream and finding out that everything he thought he had was gone.

He put his hand on the door. "Wait, Somer," he said knowing she couldn't hear him. "I love you."

## Chapter Nineteen

Overnight Somer learned more things about crying than she thought was possible. She never knew she had so many tears. She used up an entire box of tissues by the morning and was well into her second by nine A.M. That's when she decided to call in sick. No sense having to explain to everyone why her eyes were so red.

She threw on a pair of old sweatpants and an oversize New York Giants T-shirt and put a cup of water in the microwave so she could make some tea. The timer buzzed at the same time the doorbell did. It was Trent.

"I called the paper and they said you called in sick today. What's wrong?" he asked.

Somer turned and walked back into the kitchen and got her cup out of the microwave. "Nothing."

Trent followed right behind her. "With eyes as red as yours, you're fooling no one. You don't look so good."

Somer dipped a teabag into the hot water. "Thanks."

"Does it have something to do with your boyfriend bailing out of the cop swap and going back to New York?"

"I didn't think he could do that."

"He's not on our payroll. If NYPD said it was all right with them that he finishes up early, why should we care?"

"Okay then, but he's not my boyfriend."

"I beg to differ. Not the way you two acted at the awards dinner."

"I should know, Trent. I asked him to act that way."

Trent couldn't look more amazed. "I don't think he was acting."

That did it. Somer's tears burst like geyser. She covered her face with both hands and sobbed. "I know he wasn't, but he said he had to go and I let him. Now I don't know what I'm supposed to do next." She lifted her eyes and wiped her nose with the back of her hand. "You're a guy. Tell me how to get him to come back."

Trent looked stricken. "You're asking me?"

"Yes."

Trent threw up his hands. "I don't know. Once a girl breaks up with me, I usually don't want her back."

"We didn't break up," Somer said, sniffing. "We never started dating."

"So you want him to come back so you can get started."

"Yes."

"Aren't women supposed to know how to do stuff like that?"

Two spots of color appeared on Somer's cheeks. "Aren't brothers supposed to help their sisters unconditionally?"

"All right, all right," Trent said giving up. "Off the top of my head I can only think that maybe you can call and tell him you won the lottery."

Somer slumped back in her chair. "Is that the best you can come up with?"

"For the moment."

Somer's shoulders wilted a little. "If you think it would actually work, I might just consider it," she said right before she started crying again.

*What in the world am I doing?* Nick asked himself as he drove past Exit 16W on the New Jersey Turnpike. As the distance between him and Hillsborough grew longer, he felt colder, emptier. He was sure it had everything to do with leaving Somer.

So why had he? That was the question he had been trying to answer since he got on the turnpike at Exit 9 in New Brunswick.

The ache to tell her that he loved her was real. He'd told her door. That was stupid. But he couldn't tell her, and that's why he left. It was too soon, the relationship between them was virtually non-existent. Yet, when he looked to the future, everything he saw had her in it.

From the day he met her he felt like someone had hit him with a baseball bat. She stood out that day in the office. Not because she was beautiful; she was that and more. But because she had been bold enough to take him on, independent enough to take what he dished out and not bat an eye. Almost from day one he couldn't get her out of his mind, and now he didn't ever want to.

As he approached Exit 18W he knew what he had to do. He slowed the car at the tollbooth. "I'm going to make a U-turn when it's safe," he said to the toll taker.

"You can't do that. You need to go to the next exit and get back on to go the other way," the worker said.

"I know, but I have to go back right now. If you need to call the police, go ahead, but I left something very valuable for someone back in Jersey, and I have make sure the person I left it with doesn't miss it. I have to get there as soon as I can because I forgot to tell her that it's hers forever."

"What did you possibly leave that is so important that you'd risk getting arrested to just save fifteen minutes?" the toll taker asked.

"My heart," Nick replied.

The toll taker seemed to make up her mind instantly. "Well all right then," she said, looking at the emotion play on Nick's face. She reached over, flipped a switch and shut down her lane. Stepping out of the booth, she motioned for the cars behind Nick to go around as she stepped up to Nick's car and leaned into the driver's side window. "That's the only thing I would allow this for." She then proceeded to stop traffic in the other direction in the lane next to hers so Nick could turn his car around.

"I owe you," Nick said as he passed her on the southbound side of the toll.

"That you do," the worker said, seeing her boss stride angrily toward her. "That you do."

It was nearly two P.M. when Nick stepped onto the porch to Somer's house. He had called the newspaper first thinking she'd be there, but found out that she hadn't gone to work. He raised his hand and hesitated just for a moment before he knocked.

"Here goes nothing," he said with a shake of his head.

Then his knuckles hit the wood and sealed his fate.

The door opened and Somer stood there, tissue

pressed to her nose. Her eyes were red. He knew she had been crying. She gaped at him as if he were a ghost while he tried to act as though every cell in his body wasn't telling him to grab onto her.

She sniffed and opened the door wider. "Forget something?" she asked.

"Yes." For a moment he froze. Though he had rehearsed what he was going to say to her all the way down Route 287, somehow seeing how much he had hurt her actually made his heart break. "You look awful," he finally managed to get out. "Do you have a cold or something?"

"Is that all you can say to me?" She pointed to her eyes. "Do you see these? Can you tell that red is not my color?"

"You're right, and I can fix that." In one leap he threw his arms around her, nearly knocking her over before lifting her off her feet and against his chest. "I love you Somer. Love at first sight, fate, soul mates, call it whatever you want, but I love you. I should have told you as soon as I felt it, but I was stupid. We can work this out. Make time. Commute, car pool, walk, fly, swim, whatever it takes. But it will work if we let it, I know it will." He didn't give her time for an answer. His mouth crushed hers.

Her reply came non-verbally as her arms made a nest for his head and she kissed him back, their heads moving back and forth as though they could not get enough of each other. When at last she drew her head back to say, "Okay, but don't walk. You'll be too tired after you get here," her smile was as wide as the outdoors, and his was even wider. "After you left, I was afraid I'd never see you again." Tears crowded into Somer's eyes as he let her slide down the front of him with deliberate slowness.

He wiped a trailing tear from her cheek with his fingertip. "You're going to get sick of seeing me, I promise."

His beautiful eyes sparkled above the dimples she loved so much. She let her gaze travel over his face as she wound her fingers into his hair. "You made me use my last sick day," she said.

He laughed. "I'll buy you some vitamin C." His smile suddenly dropped. "Tell me you love me, Somer," he said, his eyes now dark and serious. "Because if you do, we can make this work."

"I do," she said. "But you are a cop who belongs in New York and I belong . . ."

"With me," he finished for her.

"Are you sure?"

"I am. But I told your family that you deserved to know the man you loved for more than a few weeks and I meant it. I don't have to live in the city. I'm sure there are plenty of places either near the New Jersey Turnpike or along the rail lines that are for rent."

She caught the cockiness of his smile. "You did, did you? What makes you think I'll move?"

"You don't have to. I will. I want to spend every

minute I can with you, and moving closer will help with that. I know we don't know everything about each other, so we'll take it slow. But let's start. Let's start right now."

"I have to warn you, I have a lot of bad habits," Somer cautioned. "Like I have a weakness for designer handbags. I have about fifty."

"I tend to be anal with paperwork. I bring it home and spread it out all over the living room."

"I'm a neatnik. I organize my closet according to color."

"I'm a slob. I don't use a closet much."

Somer grimaced. "I guess we'll have to work on that."

He stepped toward her, but she put up an hand to stop him. "I want to win the Pulitzer. I'm not going to stop until I do."

"I would expect nothing less."

Somer looked into his deadpan features and burst out laughing. "Are you finished?"

"There is one more thing," Nick said, "I know I don't want to be without you ever again. The rest we can figure out as we go along."

Somer's heart fluttered up into her throat. He was hers, if she wanted him. It was that simple and it was that complicated. She arched her brows. "You do know that I come with a family cast of characters that could drive away even the most steadfast of men."

"Then it should be fun at holiday time."

"You make it hard for a girl to say no."

"Then don't."

Somer laughed. "Okay. Then I can take it if you can. But don't say I didn't warn you when Mom starts planning our wedding."

"Speaking of which."

Somer gave him a wary look. "Hold on now. Knowing someone for two weeks is a little too soon for that."

"I agree. But I do remember that some of the guys back at the police station think you're pretty cute. So I think I am going to get you something so they know that you are off the market."

"Like what?"

"Like a nice, but for now, diamondless ring for your left hand until you're ready for me to replace it with something more appropriate."

Somer's face brightened as she laughed out loud. "Save your money to pay for gas for the commute. I have just the ring. Follow me."

They walked into the kitchen and Somer yanked open the freezer door. She dug into the ice cube tray, brought out the amethyst ring she'd put there and held it up between her forefinger and thumb.

"So that's the dreaded ring I've heard so much about." He held out his hand and Somer dropped it into his palm. He looked at it for a few moments.

"Seems harmless enough." He looked up at Somer. "Should we chance it?"

She held out her left hand, palm down. "I'm in."

He took the ring, slipped it onto her finger and paused for a moment. "No thunder, no lighting. I think we're okay. What do you think?"

"I think I'm glad that I went through your desk that day."

"So am I." His hand swept upward, nudging her chin up and back before his lips closed over hers.

The breath Somer didn't have time to exhale swelled in her chest. His lips didn't withdraw but brushed hers lightly back and forth, and even though she could have taken that breath now, she didn't. She was so enthralled with the feel of his lips on hers that she forgot about the need for air.

"It's funny," she whispered, kissing him between the words, "how two people . . ."

"Has anyone ever told you that you talk too much sometimes?"

His mouth came closer to hers. She felt its warmth as her breath bathed his lips. They parted and so did hers just as they touched.

About the same time an all too familiar voice came from behind them. "Don't you two have anything better to do?"

Trent had just turned the corner into the kitchen and came up short at the sight greeting him. He folded his arms across his chest and leaned against the archway, smiling and waving a piece of paper.

"I guess you don't need Nick's address in New York," he said to his sister.

"You were coming after me?" Nick asked Somer.

"Maybe," she replied with a sly smile.

Trent's gaze fell on Somer's left hand, still resting on Nick's chest. He pointed to it, eyes wide in horror. "Tell me that is not Grandma Vicky's ring on your hand."

Somer grimaced. "Sorry."

"Oh man," he said, "just don't tell Mom." Then as quickly as he entered, he turned on his heels and left. A minute later they heard the front door slam and his car start.

Alone again, Nick and Somer stared lovingly at each other. "I can't believe you were going to come to New York to find me," Nick said, letting his eyes caress her face.

"Who said I was going there to find you? Maybe I just wanted to know which Broadway show I should see first."

"I'll take you to all of them," Nick replied.

The kiss that came was different, beginning with the slow lowering of his mouth to hers. The first press of lips together built into an ardor as their hands roamed each other's backs and shoulders until they clung together as if they would never get enough.

He tore his mouth from hers only long enough to say, "I love you, Somerville Alexa Archer."

"And I love you, Nicholas Daultry."

Over his shoulder, she raised her left hand. Her grandmother's ring never looked as good as it did right now.

Made in the USA
Lexington, KY
13 April 2013